FOR GENTLEMEN ONLY

MICHAEL GYGI

author HOUSE®

AuthorHouse™
1663 Liberty Drive
Bloomington, IN 47403
www.authorhouse.com
Phone: 833-262-8899

Published by AuthorHouse 11/24/2020

ISBN: 978-1-6655-0875-9 (sc)
ISBN: 978-1-6655-0874-2 (hc)
ISBN: 978-1-6655-0873-5 (e)

Library of Congress Control Number: 2020923455

Print information available on the last page.

Dedicated to my sister Debbie who never gave up on me.

RHYTHM

Alexis, bold as Delilah, with heart true as light;
Opens up the universe that brightly beams at night.
Moving to entice in scanty lingerie,
Her softness is an asset for those who come to play.

The game is on, soon friends they'll be; the music never stops;
While quenching thirst to pass the time, another twenty drops.
A sparkling smile illuminates with words he longs to hear.
With soft sincere, she draws him near, and whispers in his ear.

Alluring spikes her strength defined; like Phoenix, again she rises
Twirling round the stable sword of gold, collecting sound stage prizes.
Seductive stirs speak silently, sweat glistens buds petite.
Inside the shadows stillness streams the flow of nectar sweat.

A private booth is empty now, only ice and glass remain;
Lipstick smeared the evidence; his trousers bear a stain.
Her dove skin hands now branch extended, tempting him to stay
For one more dance, on one more lap, all he has to do is pay.

CHAPTER 1

"**I**NVOLUNTARY MANSLAUGHTER, FIVE TO TEN YEARS. That's my offer. Take it or take your chances with a jury." Johnny sat in silence. He couldn't believe what he just heard. The district attorney made it clear that one way or another Johnny would be going to prison.

It all started five months ago with a company celebration at an Italian restaurant. The banquet room at Portello's was filled with several RayCom employees along with a diversity of aromas and the steam proliferating from the kitchen. It had been another scorcher in Los Angeles and although the air conditioning was working overtime, it was inadequate.

Ron Crocker, the manager of Technology Systems at RayCom, poured another glass of Sauvignon Blanc as he addressed the team. "Now this is what I call a Happy Hour! It took two years but we delivered. Every manager in the company labeled the CCMT project corporate suicide. That is every manager but one. You all know who I'm talking about – the one man who had the vision and skill to get the job done. The man who made CCMT a reality. Allow me to present to you the man who works miracles – our Senior Manager, Johnny Bradford."

Johnny arose from his seat at the table. The lights from the ceiling fans brought out the distinguished grey streaks on his temples. The decibel level reached its threshold as he gave everyone the thumbs' up. Johnny smiled as he eyed his teammates.

"You did it." He continued to praise the ensemble in fine cliché fashion. "I can't spell success without 'U'," as his fingers drew the letter in the air.

The cheering and applause continued to build. Everyone in the room knew of Johnny's sincerity even if he was a bit old-fashioned. Johnny was a traditionalist. Always pressed shirt and tie along with a sport coat. The polish on his shoes was fresh. One couldn't tell if Johnny was wearing new shoes or if he just came from the shine booth on 9th street. Johnny always kept a small can of wax polish, an applicator dauber, shine brush and a soft cotton buff cloth in his bottom desk drawer. Johnny didn't care if he was dealing with maintenance or CEOs; he wanted to look his professional best.

His art of negotiation was without equal. Johnny said there would be work enough for everyone and didn't concede to let one supplier manage all the work.

When Johnny accepted the assignment for the CCMT project, his non-aggressive plan was met with much dissention. He had a high success rate despite his conservative approach. He was always ethical and above board. His superiors agreed he was an effective manager but had concerns whether or not Johnny was progressive and keeping up with the demands for new and more efficient technology.

There had been rumors that deliverables and deployments had not always been put together the way the company wanted and possibly members of Johnny's team had cut corners. Human resources had been brought in to look into possible violations of company policies or best practices, but no evidence had ever been found to substantiate the rumors. Those close to Johnny said it was professional jealousy that others were trying to get a leg up on him or stab him in the back.

As focused as he was to schedule and budget, these were not his top priorities. Johnny's agenda was to see the team members grow, pull together and succeed. He would challenge them to do more than they thought capable.

He seemed to know exactly what was needed from every vantage point whether it was finance, engineering, manufacturing, or information systems. He also knew how to assemble a team that collectively comprised the skills needed to complete a project. But more importantly, he always created a team that could work together.

Johnny continued to distribute accolades. He mentioned there would be a nice little company reward for each of them. He then made his way around the table shaking hands with everyone along with a gratuitous back slap to the more raucous team members.

As the perspiring waiters brought everyone more appetizers and hors d'oeuvres, Johnny took his seat next to Ron. Ron Crocker was Johnny's right hand man and senior technical lead for operations. Although Ron was a first line manager, he spent more time with his sleeves rolled up in the technology rather managing the business and leading the other team members. He left that to Johnny.

One of the team members called out above all the noise, "Hey Johnny, I hope you're getting a nice bonus for this!" Johnny smiled and replied, "I have a feeling you folks are eating it right now! The boss told me to do something nice for you folks. This is what I chose. I hope he wasn't thinking of coffee mugs with his face on them!"

The roar of laughter was seeping out into the restaurant. The Portello's patrons were envious they hadn't been invited to the party. Johnny had a sense of humor but kept it pretty low key most of the time. Although Johnny was usually all business, his employees enjoyed it when he would make light of something.

For those who didn't know Johnny or had never worked with him, their first impression probably would have been that Johnny was as serious as a heart attack. Employees saw him as very professional as well as approachable. Johnny was engaged with his employees while at work but it ended there. He was not anti-social, but he chose not to mingle with employees after hours. He kept his personal life to himself. There were employees who had no idea he was married since he didn't wear a ring. There were no pictures of his wife or family in his office. The fact that he was celebrating with the group was unprecedented.

As the dining and revelry began to diminish, Ron pulled Johnny aside and congratulated him personally on a great achievement.

"Thanks for picking me to run the technical side of the house. I was afraid you might not pick me. We're more than peers and everyone knows that our friendship extends beyond work. I thought maybe you might be worried about, well you know, favoritism."

"Nonsense," replied Johnny, "I chose you because you were the best man for the job. Friendship had nothing to do with it. I wouldn't care if you were green and had horns. You knew all the finite technical details that I didn't understand. You understood the technology and you knew how to incorporate it into the product. That is why I chose you. Oh, one more thing, I knew you would get the job done."

Ron was right to have concerns about preference whether or not it had the appearance of bias. He had been the technical lead on several projects much to the chagrin of some other employees who felt they had been overlooked. He was extremely knowledgeable in all of the technical areas: engineering, analysis, programming and infrastructure. He was strong compliment to Johnny's high level enterprise understanding and business acumen. Everyone seemed to rely on Ron's technical insight and would go forward with his recommendations.

Joe Bordan as he made his way back to the celebration. There was a Montecristo cloud still clinging to him. His satisfied grin displayed the yellow tinge of his teeth which hid his once white enamel in the same manner as the hovering grey haze over the L.A. basin hid the San Bernardino Mountains. Joe was extremely intelligent and was considered by many to be the best technician in the company.

Joe could do anything but chose to spend the majority of his time finding ways to get other folks to do the work while he would accept the credit. Although Joe's work ethic was questionable, his skill was not. He had solved numerous technical problems that had baffled the other technicians in the group.

The noise level in the banquet room was decreasing with the culmination of the happy hour appetizers and hors d'oeuvres. The ravioli, stuffed mushrooms and wine were nothing more than a palatable memory. Some of the team members were already on their way home firing up a jump start to the weekend ahead. Cord Williams, Paul Miller and Joe joined Ron and Johnny at the table to discuss plans for the rest of the evening. Joe, holding a wine glass in his hand, offered Johnny an invitation.

"We're getting ready to head out to the gentleman's club if you would like to join us."

"You mean they still have those? Just a special place for us guys where we can go relax, read a book, enjoy a brandy, game of chess and no women to bother us?"

"You're kidding, right?" asked Cord.

"Yes, I'm kidding," replied Johnny. "So, are you all heading out to the Chaise?"

"You bet," said Joe; "Are you coming?"

"No," Johnny replied.

"Have you ever been there?" Joe asked.

"No." Johnny stated with pride.

Joe's cross-examination continued, "Have you ever been to any Gentleman's Club?"

Johnny shook his head.

"I do not believe it, we have got a virgin here!" exclaimed Cord, "Now you have got to come. Let us see that you are treated right!"

Johnny smiled at the excited gang, "No thanks boys, not my cup of tea. Don't let me spoil your fun. Go out and have a good time and stay out of trouble. What about you Paul, are you going?"

"No way Johnny! I can't see spending time in a place that gets me horny as hell and sends me home broke with nothing to show for it!" Paul put up his hands surrendering to the group's laughter and whooping. Even Johnny seemed to be joining in with their frivolity.

With a wave of their hands Cord and Joe started out to the parking lot. Their journey in search of momentary intimate pleasures was now underway. Pleasures that could only be found at the Chaise as long as their wallets were full.

As Paul headed towards the door, he looked back at Ron and Johnny and said,

"It does not matter how a place is dressed up or whatever name it chooses to be known by. There is still a stage decorated with colored lights where half naked, beautiful women remove what little clothing they have for you suckers."

Ron waved his hand to Cord and Joe as they left Portello's. As Ron turned his head, Johnny made eye contact with him and asked, "Are you going?"

"Sure, why not? It's not like I'm planning on hooking up with someone and getting lucky. It's just a way of winding down for me. From my point of view, it is kind of like going to the movies, except this is more of an interactive virtual reality, if you know what I mean."

Johnny sighed, "I don't see it that way; it's porn, live porn and it's wrong. I don't know if I could look at my wife again after going there. I'm pretty open-minded but it just doesn't seem right for a guy like me to go to a place like that."

"So it's OK for a guy like me to go to a place like that?" questioned Ron with a grin.

"Not at all. You know what I mean." Johnny answered.

"Yes I do", confirmed Ron. "Well I'm going to head out and join Cord, Joe and the other gentlemen who are already unwinding. I tell you what Johnny, if you change your mind and need to escape the pressure and loosen up a little, here is a pass. No cover; save you $20.00.

Johnny stared down at the card with raise eyebrows, "You a regular?"

"Not really," Ron winked, "I know a couple of people who work there. Thanks again for the party. I'll see you bright and early Monday morning."

Johnny put the card into his wallet and drove home. He had told his wife Jenny not to worry about fixing dinner since he would be out celebrating with the team. He was looking forward to just sitting down on the couch and telling her all about it. As he opened his front door, there was a look of confusion on his face as he noticed his grandchildren sitting on the couch in the living room being read to by Jenny.

"It's after 7:30. Shouldn't they have gone home a couple of hours ago?" Jenny recognizing her husband's surprise explained, "Maddy and Jim needed some time together and wanted to go out for dinner and a movie so I offered to watch the kids."

"I see." Johnny leaned over the couch and kissed Jenny on the forehead. He then opened up his arms and both boys scooted closer together on either side of Jenny for him to hug.

"I'm going into the back and read a little," he said softly. "Fine", answered Jenny, "The kids should be gone by around 10:30 and after that I just want to go to bed if that's alright. It's been a long day and the heat didn't make it any easier to deal with."

"I understand. I'm sure you've had a busy day."

Johnny carefully made his way to the back room where his office was located while avoiding stepping on trucks, dinosaurs and blocks that were scattered about creating an obstacle course.

Here was his sanctuary; it was the one room in the house where the grandchildren were not allowed. Here Johnny could relax in his recliner, turn on his music and read one of his books or trade magazines while enjoying a glass of wine. This is what he lived for.

While Johnny listened to Dvorak's New World Symphony, he thought of how exciting it must have been for Dvorak to come to America and see a world he had only heard of and read about. A world so different from his own that it inspired him to compose one of his greatest works.

Johnny's persona was a paradox. Although he was somewhat content with his current lifestyle, he thought about what it would be like to see another world and become a different person. A person who commanded respect when he entered a room. A man that the ladies looked up to and wanted to know better. A world that could excite and enliven him. A world where he would escape from the drab, uneventful home life he had been living. He wanted more than just his music and books at night.

He looked at the card inside his wallet and wondered if this was the passport to the world he was looking for. He thought of what a hypocrite he would be showing up at the club after expressing his disdain for it. He wondered if his co-workers would think differently of him and see him as immoral. He resigned himself to the fact that they invited him, so they most likely wouldn't think of him differently.

He walked back into the living room where Jenny was now deep into one of her gothic novels. The grandchildren were in sleeping bags on the living room carpet, peacefully slumbering with halos above their heads.

"The guys from work invited me to join them at this club," Johnny said awkwardly.

"Enjoy. As you can see, Maddy and Jim aren't back yet. I'll probably be in bed by the time you get home. By the way, I'm taking David and Jonathan to a petting zoo tomorrow."

Johnny kissed her forehead again "I'll see you in a while." He approached his car as if setting sail on an expedition to uncharted lands.

CHAPTER 2

————————————●

I T IS NOT UNUSUAL TO SEE more than 200 cars in the Chaise parking lot on a Friday night. Also, it's not unusual to see a couple of the Chaise girls having a nightcap at the Stagger, a sordid bar one step above a dive about half a mile down the road from the Chaise. Nor is it unusual to find automobiles of all classes at the Easy 8 Motel directly across the street from the Stagger that rented rooms by the hour. But it was unusual to see a pristine 1965 Ford Mustang pulling into the Chaise parking lot. Not that the car was so unusual, it was its driver, Johnny Bradford.

Johnny found an open spot at the far end of the parking lot which possessed the only street lights in that industrial neighborhood. This was primarily for the girls' protection. Discretion wasn't really a consideration, nor was it a problem.

The Chaise referred to itself as a gentlemen's club, as if that would cover that fact that it was nothing more than a strip joint. Although the Chaise catered to the respectful businessman who could be seen wearing coat and tie while sipping on a Bombay Sapphire martini, there were also men of other class distinctions. This include the beer drinking, unshaven, crude language, dirty jeans and T-shirt men.

The inside walls were garnished with imitation art of nudes. Microfiber couches, booths and chairs complemented the comfort and style of even the most discerning tastes. There was even valet parking for the more than 200 gentlemen who needed an atmosphere of discretion and relaxation. All of this for the small cover charge of $20.00.

There were big screens televisions with sporting events mounted over the bar. On one of the walls adjacent to the stage, there were projected silhouettes of unrecognizable naked women dancing. This provided an addition appetite wetting for the patrons.

Everything was above-board at the Chaise. Soliciting was not allowed, and some customers were actually removed from time to time for making such inquiries. There was talk that occasionally one of the Chaise girls might meet up with a patron at another location for a drink or two and go off together, though Chase management denied that sort of activity ever occurred.

Girls who worked at the Chaise could make anywhere from a couple hundred to a thousand dollars a night. It was all about playing the right mark. There were regulars who had their special girls and thought nothing of dropping a couple hundred or more to be made to feel as if they were something special for 30 minutes to an hour.

Gentlemen could get a lap dance at their seat for $20.00. There were also private booths behind the couch area adjacent to the stage for $30.00 a dance. The Chaise also offered private rooms, affectionately referred to as the "naughty rooms," starting at $300.00 for 30 minutes, complete with a bottle of wine. There was also 15 minutes for $150.00 for those of lesser financial means.

For those of much more discriminating taste, there was an hour in a private room, complete with a chilled bottle of Dom Pérignon and Beluga caviar. All for the very competitive price of $1500. As long as men have money and are willing to pay, they can enjoy their fantasies and the Chaise will continue to flourish.

Access to the Chaise was monitored by a proud sentinel. He was a rather large man whose polo shirt sleeves hugged his barbed wired tattooed biceps as he folded his arms across his chest. The girls all referred to him as Sweets. He was not just the bouncer, he was also part owner and he loved being the enforcer when the situation called for such action.

As Johnny walked through the entrance, a deep voice told him to put out his arms. Sweets' bulky calloused hands patted Johnny down. A sudden sense of guilt came to him during this ritual. This was the sort of procedure he thought to be reserved for the criminal element of society, not upstanding citizens such as himself. Johnny reconciled his conscience with the fact that he wasn't doing anything wrong, at least that was the justification that Ron argued.

With his mind at ease, he handed the frisking monolith the pass Ron had given him and passed through the velvet portals leaving reality behind and unlocking the door to fantasy.

Johnny's pupils immediately dilated upon passing through the velvet curtains. He was in total darkness, or so it seemed. For a moment he thought he was blind. Within a few seconds he silently rejoiced as his eyesight was restored. He could now make out the stage with the spot lights rotating colors to the music. Johnny continued to search in vain through the crowded booths and tables for his friends.

Johnny's eyes were not alone in the disarray. His ears were victims as well. The only sound emanating was the booming bass of the DJ's sound system setting the appropriate atmosphere for the dancers to entice their gentleman guests. If there truly was music being played, Johnny thought it undiscernible. Besides the decibel level, it was music that Johnny wasn't the least bit familiar with or moved by.

Johnny awkwardly made his way through the crowd trying not to accidentally bump a waitress who might be carrying a full tray of long necks. The club floor was overflowing with seductively dressed girls ranging in ages from 19 to 40. It was a difficult challenge to divert his attention away from them and remain focused on the problem at hand: finding a seat. He stopped before reaching the stage. He thought he heard his name being called but wasn't sure due to the thundering sound that engulfed him. He turned to the left and saw Cord, Joe and Ron waving their arms.

Joe hollered to Johnny in an unfamiliar vernacular. Johnny was not accustomed to hearing the men he worked with swear or curse since their business environment was professional and Johnny did little socializing with them outside of work. He was seeing a side of his co-workers he had never seen before and it made him uneasy. He thought it interesting that these men could change as though they had stepped through a portal to another universe that reconfigured their personalities. A portal that he himself had walked through which opened the door to his own future change.

Johnny made his way through the patrons and stretched out his hand to Ron who pulled Johnny into the booth and hollered, "The place is pretty packed. I'm surprised you found a place to park! What are you drinking? Good grief man, what are you doing with your coat on? It's still eighty degrees outside!"

"I'll have a beer. You know this is how I dress. Besides, I think it might cool down later. Anyway, I came here to relax, but with all this noise and so many people, I don't know if I can. I had no idea this place was so huge!"

"Don't worry about it," said Ron. "You will get used to it. Sit back, enjoy a cold one and let your eyes partake of paradise. At least my view of paradise!" Ron chuckled.

Joe motioned to one of the waitresses and slurred out what sounded like, "Bring this man a beer. He is thirsty! And he is a hero!" The waitress nodded and went back to the bar.

"So, how did you get away and what changed your mind?" Ron inquired.

"Like I said, I felt I really needed to relax and that wasn't going to happen at home. Jenny was busy with the grandkids and they had left their land mines all over the house. You know how I can be when things are just scattered and cluttered!"

"Oh you mean like the way you just shake your head every time you see Joe's desk?" interrupted Cord.

"Yes, just like that. Well as I was saying, I wanted to share the excitement we had generated earlier at Portello's with Jenny and make her a part of it. But the timing just wasn't right. It's not her fault and I don't blame her, I was just hoping to share something of mine with her. She was pretty preoccupied and was going to call it a night soon anyway. I was a little let down and I kept looking at the pass you gave me and thought maybe you guys could raise my spirits a little."

"And that's not all we will raise," laughed Cord. "You've done so much for us; let us give you back a little sign of our gratitude. Oh look, here comes your beer." Joe stood up and handed the waitress a ten dollar bill. "Keep it," he said. The waitress nodded once, said thank you with an appreciative smile.

Johnny took a sip of his beer, "I can't believe how attractive all the girls are here. I mean they don't look cheap or sleazy, you know what I mean? I wasn't sure what to expect."

"I've got news for you," said Ron, "They aren't cheap. Some of these girls will take home over a grand tonight. Some of them have already scoped out the sugar daddies and are making their play. Others are cuddling with their regulars – at least for as long as the money holds out, and then they'll move on to someone else."

"You make them out to be so cold and callous", remarked Johnny.

"Well they are. What we see are soft, gentle and caring women. That is what we want and why we come here in the first place. Though they are beautiful on the outside, we know they are condescending to us on the inside. We know we would never have a chance with girls that look like this, but for the little bit of time we're in here, they make us believe it's so, and we pay. It's just business.

Come on Johnny, we are just as cold and callous in our business dealings. Think about it. When we bid on a contract, we are convincing the potential customers that we will deliver our highest quality work at the best price. The customers likes what they hear and buy into the sales sleaze. And speaking of contracts, how about our former executive vice president and his senior project manager getting a hold of our competitors' bid? After they analyze it, they manage to come up with a more attractive bid for the contract. They get caught and we have to go to ethics training!

You know as well as I do that we could do much of the work ourselves and put the best quality into all of it. The reality is we will sub-contract much of what is to be done to a supplier who is cheaper and their product just meets the constraints of quality.

We talk about how important our people are but when the bottom line is in trouble, many of the highly skilled, senior employees received an unexpected low assessment. When it's time for lay-offs, the higher salaries get the notices. In the end there is no difference between the way we run our business and how the girls run theirs. It's all about the money."

"How can you even compare what we do to this? What they do is immoral!" stammered Johnny.

"And your telling me business isn't?" argued Ron. "As far as I am concerned, money exchanged with profit in mind without concern for the customer is immoral. At least I know what I am going to get when I come in here and how much it is going to cost me. There is no pretense, I just sit back and enjoy the evening. For me, that is not immoral. It is just like going to a live show where there is a little bit of public interaction."

"You know Ron, you sound just as cold and callous as the women you are describing. You are probably right. There are women like that in here just looking to get as much as they can; no emotion, no regrets. But I believe there are a few women here who may be here due to extraneous circumstances. They may have made bad decisions and are now paying the price. Maybe they feel their only resort is to use what God gave them while they still have it. They sense nothing else is available to them; at least for the kind of money that is available. I believe there are even some here who actually feel for the gentlemen they entertain. Whether planned or not sometimes chemistry ignites and it becomes more than a dancer/ patron relationship."

"Well my friend, you couldn't have summarized it better if you were standing at the pulpit on Sunday morning." Johnny smiled at Ron and held up his beer bottle and waiting to clink Ron's.

At the opposite end of the club near the pool table stood three of Chaise's beauties. Diamond, Phoenix and a new girl, Baby were all surveying the club in hopes of another victim. All three ladies were what could only be described as opulent 'eye candy'. Their shapely arms led eyes to the tips of their scarlet fingernails. Their well-proportioned figures were supported by long tan legs, without stockings. Diamond and Phoenix had breasts that would pay tribute to Beverly Hills most affluent plastic surgeons. The ladies' lace lingerie added an illusion of elegance and left little to the imagination.

Phoenix had been eyeing Johnny since his arrival. His awkwardness and professional appearance made him a potential target. Joe watched as Phoenix made her move to their table. Johnny had no idea that the firebird was looking to engulf another victim in her erotic inferno. Johnny was still in a conversation with Ron, totally oblivious to the flames that were creeping towards him. A soft delicate hand with long fingers tousled Johnny's hair. A mild tone and delicate voice asked, "Would you like some company hun?"

A startled Johnny grabbed for the table as he fell out of his seat. Ron and Phoenix quickly grabbed a hold of Johnny's arms while Joe stood laughing hysterically. They lifted him back up.

"A little jumpy, huh sugar?" Phoenix teased.

"That's not fair", Johnny remarked with hesitation and embarrassment. "You caught me off my guard."

Phoenix curled her upper lip seductively. She pressed herself against his arm and spoke right outside his ear with a soft inflection. "Well it's seems to me you're wound up a little too tight. You need to relax. How about if I keep you company for a while?"

Johnny tried to find the words for refusal but he was tongue-tied. Before he could respond, Joe handed Phoenix a $20 bill and hollered, "I give you the virgin, bring me back the man!"

"A virgin," replied Phoenix?

"I'm a first timer," said Johnny sheepishly.

The music transitioned to what Johnny could only define as lost jungle vibrations finding their way to the inner city angst. Even though the song had a definitive overbearing beat which drowned out any possibility of a recognizable melody, there was something about it that pulled Johnny in as the syncopated gyrations of Phoenix now commanded his attention.

She placed one spiked heel on Johnny's chair with her knee knocking up against his chest. She loosened his tie as she pulled his head forward and ran her claws through his hair. She breathed softly into his ear rubbing her cheek against his. She quickly turned with her back facing Johnny. She bent over and shook her buttocks and spanked herself with one hand. Ron and Cord applauded while whistling in extreme delight.

"I knew she would give him his money's worth!" Joe exclaimed

"You mean your money's worth." Cord replied.

"Aw, who cares?" retorted Joe. "Hey he is having a good time." Cord left his seat and started walking toward the far stage. He looked back at his friends, "I'm going to head over to the other end; I want to check out that Asian chick."

Ron thought Johnny looked like a statue interacting with a machine while Phoenix went through her motions. Her sensual moves seemed all too choreographed and repetitive. Probably the same routine she had gone through with other customers. As the song wound to its end, Phoenix put both her hands on Johnny's shoulders and asked, "How about another hun?" Johnny looked into her eye and replied, "I think one will do me."

"OK, thanks", were her last words as she was off in search of another hapless victim who was willing to pay the price of lap dance nirvana.

Johnny sat up in his chair looking like man who was trying to regain his composure without looking like he lost it. Ron patted him on the back and asked, "Well what did you think?"

"Although I wasn't comfortable at first, I am embarrassed to say that as the song went on and I was looking at her, I enjoyed it. I'm going to have another drink, you boys going to join me?" Ron shook his head. "I'm outta here Johnny. I've had enough fun for one night. I'll see you on Monday."

Ron moved forward from the booth and stood up. He caught Joe's attention and waved to him. Joe acknowledged and decided to head out the door with Ron. The two men left the Chaise, leaving Johnny sitting alone.

CHAPTER 3

THE LIONESS PROWLS IN THE HIGH grass. She is confident and stays hidden. It is not unusual to see several lionesses hunting together where they can encircle a herd from different angles. A lioness is patient; she will study all her potential victims for some time before making a decision. She's careful not to choose one too fast or too strong. She knows she has to make her strike count. She moves subtly through the savannah grass and she draws closer to her unsuspecting prize. She has a tendency to choose large mammals who are slow.

The Chaise is well known for the lionesses that prowl its premises. They are most active after dark and tend to spend a good deal of their time socializing and grooming. They, like their feline counterparts, stalk the herd of adult males. Men who overeat, and consume large quantities of alcohol and get by with little or no physical exertion. Men who know for the right price, they can be just as appealing as the cats they are eyeing. The cats of predation are quick to ascertain the lonely, the forgotten and the deprived. Where diminishing self-esteem is observed, the cats will prowl and skulk.

Diamond was such a lioness. She was older than she looked and could easily pass for twenty-five. Although thirty-eight wouldn't be considered aged, but as in professional sports, a stripper's career is usually over by the time she hits forty. Diamond took care of herself or at least she saw to it she was well taken care of. She always had complimentary passes to the local gyms and health clubs. She ate well, drank little outside of the Chaise and never smoked.

Diamond observed the bump and grind show given by Phoenix with interest and thought to herself, "Oh my God, another rerun." She had seen Phoenix go through her routine on numerous occasions, never wavering, never changing, and never getting a second dance. The experienced dancers always saw the opportunities the minor ones overlooked. This time it was a victim who needed to be needed.

Johnny flagged a waitress and ordered another drink; this time, a margarita on the rocks.

Johnny was an occasional drinker and not one to ever get intoxicated. The elevated volume with which he had to speak to Ron at Chaise along with the blistering heat of the day had left him a bit parched. He let out a deep sigh as the cool citrus liquor soothed his desiccated throat. He loved the taste of a good drink, especially ice cold. He was a sipper; he could make one drink last all night.

He loved holding the glass in his hand and swirling the ice inside. It gave him a sense of power and prestige. In Johnny's mind, the way a man held his drink said a great deal about the man; the same way a man stands upright or holds his head. As each new dancer took her turn on the stage, Johnny took another sip; and with each sip he clenched his teeth and pulled his lips back tight in true Bogart style as if this brought out the inner man inside him.

Johnny wanted to release that inner man. A man of excitement, impulse and strength. A man whose character was enticing to women. That is the way he wanted to be seen, and that's the façade he would try to present. But deep down, there was one thing missing in Johnny's life that he wanted more than anything else: to be loved. At least to feel as though he was loved.

He felt his life was nothing more than numbers and growth, such as the business at RayCom. It was all so superficial. He wanted just once for a woman to see him as a man, an attractive man. An exciting man that was as mysterious and complex as the universe in which he lived. He would give anything to have one woman love him the way he wanted to be loved. He would make her the center of his world and nothing else would matter because of their love. He loved his wife Jenny and knew she loved him, even though it was not the way he wanted to be loved. He became lost in his own complicated and contradictory delusions.

Johnny's movements were still under the watchful eye of Diamond.

Johnny was totally unaware that he was being observed. At first he wasn't aware of any one dancer, waitress or particular customer at the Chaise. Then his eyes caught the dancer on the stage. He was amazed at the strength she had pulling herself up the pole on center stage. At one point she straddled her the pole with her legs and spun around several times. She then turned upside down and slowly spun till her head reached the stage and she pulled herself upright. Johnny expected her to look muscular but in fact she looked quite feminine.

Then Johnny found himself overwhelmed with all the activity going on around him. The bar maids, the lap dances, the music and the dancers were too distracting for him to focus on any one action. Everything going on around him became a blur.

Diamond recognized his lack of concentration and started establishing her advance. She walked over to Baby, a young, petite Vietnamese girl. She discretely pointed over to where Johnny was sitting.

"See that daddy over there? The one that Phoenix left unchanged?" Baby nodded. Diamond continued, "Well since you're new, young and impressionable, I'm going to give you an education. Phoenix does it all wrong and that's why she doesn't get many repeat customers. It's rare that they would ask her to stay awhile, have a drink and chat. She doesn't know how to read them. You need to know how to read your guy so you know what to expect. Then you deliver."

"I not understand", said Baby with her strong accent, "Don't they all want same thing?"

"Sure they do but they all want it differently. Look at that guy over there in the sleeveless t-shirt and tattoos – a testosterone octopus on steroids! You'll spend all your time pushing his hands back on the chair where they belong, never mind the dance. And that geek boy with the plaid shirt buttoned up to the top. He'll spend the entire time sitting on his hands, wide-eye and gawking. He probably won't notice your dance movements. Make sure you wipe up the drool when you're done."

"And then there's the 'I want more guy'. He's always willing to pay more to get more – if you get my drift. He's pretty sharp. He doesn't come out and ask for sex because he knows that's illegal. When you ask if he would like another dance, he will say something like, "Oh, most definitely, but isn't there another place we could go that is a little more private?" Well we all know the rules and some girls bend them a little even though there are risks. Remember, with risks there can be payoffs, but also there are letdowns and consequences. I try to keep my risks minimal."

Diamond continued, "You'll be able to pick out who has potential and who doesn't soon enough. But right now, while you are learning the ropes, pay attention to the girls more than the gentlemen."

"What you mean Diamond?" Baby's face was puzzled.

Diamond pointed to the stage.

"First watch the dancers. See which girls are getting money tossed up on the stage. If there seems to be more money on the stage than usual and a good crowd of guys at the front, you need to know why. Listen to her music. Are the gents into her song selections? Watch her movements. Are they smooth, sharp, different from the other girls? Is there a smile on her face or eye contact? Is there any interaction with the guys up front? Does she give the impression she is dancing just for their eyes and are they eating her up? Is there anything unique about the way she removes her clothes or where she places them?"

Baby listened attentively as if she were in school. "Now most important, once she comes back into the crowd, does she sit among those who have shown their appreciation with money on the stage, does she immediately get asked for a lap dance, a private dance or does she have to hustle a bit?"

Baby's mind soaked it all in like a new sponge, Diamond concluded, "Now I know we don't make much on the stage, but the stage is where we cast out our line and see if they will take the bait. We're here to make money and there's more to be made on their laps than there is on the stage."

A half smile worked its way around the corners of Baby's mouth as Diamond reassured her with a wink. Diamond felt it was her role to be mentor and guide Baby along rather than let her figure it out on her own along with the bad experiences inexperience can bring.

"I guess you seen them all."

"You bet I have and I'm not the type to get stung twice. We're all here to play the game and I know all too well when the game's gone on long enough and it's time to get out! It's a lot like fishing."

Diamond looked up into Baby's eyes and smiled. "First you've got to have the right bait. Not all fish like the same bait. When one does bite, don't pull too quickly, you'll pull the bait and hook right out of his mouth and he gets away. The trick is to let him nibble a little bit and once he has bitten off too much, you hook him! Of course you'll play with him while he puts up a fight all the while you are reeling him in slowly until he's finished. Now take daddy over there; an appeal to his vanity will be the bait, and submitting to it will be his fate."

Diamond's countenance was animated. Baby was impressed with her confidence. "Pay attention and learn Miss Baby." Diamond picked up an empty glass from the table in front her. She grinned, and gave Baby another wink as she walked over towards the booth where Johnny was sitting alone.

Johnny was wondering what the dancers perception of him was. Only Phoenix has come up and talked to him. He thought maybe he just looked like some old man who came for a peep show. He hardly noticed when Diamond sat down next to him and slipped her feet out of her three inch spiked heels.

"I hope you don't mind, my feet are killing me. When I stand too long in once place it really takes a toll on my back and my feet. I need to keep moving if you know what I mean."

Johnny tightened up the knot in his tie and cinched it back under his collar. He rotated his neck to relieve some of the stiffness of the long day. He then proceeded to work his hair back in place with his fingers. Before Johnny could answer, Diamond spoke up again, "I just need to unwind for a few if you don't mind."

"No, I don't mind." Johnny paused and started to converse. "So how's business for you tonight?"

"Well if you really want to know, only fair tonight, but then again I haven't really worked it yet. So far all I've had are hicks and gropers."

Johnny laughed, "Hicks and gropers. What in the world..."

Diamond was quick to enlighten, "Gropers, you know those guys whose hands are everywhere except where they are supposed to be, down at their sides. And hicks, I'm sure you've seen them? They are the golly, aw shucks ma'am types who are still in their work clothes and didn't think it mattered if they washed up or not after changing the oil! And I'm still working on my cover."

"Cover, what's that?" Johnny interrupted, "are you talking about a different job or assignment?"

"Oh no hun, the minute a girl walks into the club for her shift, she antes up one hundred dollars. None of the dancers are on the payroll; the money we make is from tips and only tips. That's why the girls use a lot of pressure when they first start their shift. Once they make their cover, they can relax a little more and don't mind spending time with the clientele."

Diamond's relaxed and open dialogue about Chaise customers and management put Johnny at ease. He imagined he could tell her anything and she would find it interesting. He could see her engaged in the conversation contributing commentary that he could relate to. And likewise she would be tuned-in to his observations as well. Johnny raised his glass for another sip; Diamond raised hers in unison as though she was toasting her new found provider. Johnny hadn't noticed that her glass was empty as she pretended to put down her last swallow. In fact, he had not even noticed the lingerie she was wearing.

Her sheer net robe dropped over her shoulders while accentuating her model-like figure. Her long tan legs begged to be touched. The only thing Johnny noticed was the crimson sculptured pedicure of her pampered toes that dangled from her bare foot as her leg swung in rhythm while she spoke. Johnny leaned closer to Diamond and asked, "So, are you close to making cover?"

"Getting there. I haven't tried too hard yet and I've still got a little over three hours to go."

"You're here until two in the morning?" Johnny asked.

"It's no big deal", Diamond replied, "I'm used to it. I go back to my apartment, unwind for a bit, crash on my bed and sleep like a rock."

"When do you get up and start your day, if you don't mind my asking", probed Johnny.

"Not at all, 'round two or three in the afternoon."

Johnny now took his first serious look at Diamond. His eyes took him everywhere. As he drank in her beauty, he once more thought of Dvorak and the New World motivation, which led inescapably to revisiting his own desire for a New World adventure."

Her auburn hair draped over her lightly tanned shoulders that highlighted a few freckles. She occasionally gave her hair a soft toss suggesting she had a wild side. Her dark eyes added to her mystery. She was approachable and alluring. He enjoyed Diamond's company and conversation. He was at ease with her and felt no impending pressure.

"You know I wasn't planning on coming here tonight, but I was curious, never having been in an establishment like this and then once I arrived, I knew I wasn't going to stay long. But now, after talking with you I feel I have a reason to stay." Johnny looked down at his empty glass. "Will you have a drink with me?"

"What a nice thing to say, you're such a sweetheart. What's your name hun?"

"I'm sorry, I wasn't thinking. John," he paused, "But everyone calls me Johnny. And yours?"

"I'm Diamond."

"A gem if ever I saw one", replied Johnny with sincerity.

"Aren't you the clever one!" laughed Diamond. "It's not like I haven't heard similar lines, but I like it just the same."

Johnny flagged the waitress over, "I'll have another and um, what will you have"?

"Tanqueray on the rocks with a cranberry chaser." She smiled at her waitress. "That's nice of you Johnny. I'm still thirsty and they always keep it a little warm in here. I don't know if it's because the girls aren't wearing much or if it's just another enticement to get the customers to drink more."

While the waitress made her way to the bar, Diamond took a hold of Johnny's hand.

"You know you seem like a really nice guy. Tell me all about yourself. So far I've done all the talking, maybe that's why I'm so thirsty."

There was a long pause, Johnny was drawing a blank. He couldn't remember the last time someone wanted to know about him and his interests. Part of the problem was Johnny was still trying to understand himself.

He thought about his being a professional manager with a score of successes to his credit and a pat resume. He saw himself as a dutiful husband as well as a loving father and doting grandfather. But deep inside there was also the suppressed free spirit of adventure.

Johnny longed to be seen as a confident ladies man. A man of control and power. Johnny certainly was confident when managing a project or a team. He carried himself well when it came time to get commitments and negotiate deliverables and schedule. But to Johnny, these challenges were easy to work. A beautiful woman was something altogether different and frightening. Johnny smiled and acknowledged Diamond's hand in his. "I'm married", he said, "Thirty-five years' worth."

"My, that's quite a milestone", interrupted Diamond.

"I am a simple kind of guy I guess. Life in the suburbs, a religious wife who volunteers for everything. Oh, and I like volunteering too."

"I work my five days a week and enjoy my solitude and music when I can get it." Johnny stopped for a moment as if trying to describe himself in more detail. He then spoke up again. "I guess that's about it, not much to tell."

By now the waitress was back with the cocktails. "That'll be twenty-five dollars," she said looking at Johnny.

Johnny stammered, "Twenty-five dollars? The last drink I had was seven dollars, how much is it now?"

"Yours is still seven, the drinks you ordered for your guest come to eighteen," the waitress replied.

"Wow", exclaimed Johnny. "How come hers cost so much more?"

"The girls' drinks always cost more," the waitress replied. "That's just the way it is."

Johnny reached into his front pocket and pulled out his money clip. He thumbed through and removed a twenty and a five. He handed the money to the waitress and put his hand and money clip back in his pocket. Diamond looked at Johnny as she nudged her head towards the waitress with eyes opened wide at him with a stare that begged the question, "Didn't you forget something?" Johnny paused while shaking his head while retrieving the money clip once again and gave the waitress two dollars.

"Thank ya darlin'. Let me know if you need anything else." And with that the waitress moved on to the next dehydrated client.

Diamond picked up her glass of gin and held it waiting for Johnny to toast with her. Johnny obliged and brought his glass up to hers.

"Here's to new friends", said Diamond as she gave Johnny's glass a clink.

This was the seal of approval Johnny had been hoping for. He felt Diamond truly accepted him as a friend and not just another patron.

"Boy, I needed that," she said as she put the empty shot glass back down on the table. "I just know there's more to you than you think there is. Come on; tell me what you do for fun?"

Johnny thought back to the activities he enjoyed when he was a younger man, activities he and his wife participated in together. In their early marriage, hiking through canyons and national parks were their passions. He described how he and Jenny used to lie underneath the stars together once the night's cloud cover had disappeared and gaze at the infinite opulence and grandeur.

Johnny remembered their Labrador who was always with them on their hikes, chasing and retrieving whatever rocks or sticks they may have found along the trek.

"I love to dance and used to be pretty good with a waltz and a swing. I could see myself as a handsome, dashing romantic lead straight out of Hollywood's golden era gliding across a dance floor with a beautiful woman following my every step like Astaire & Rogers. There were times when I would go to clubs for a little swing dancing but never felt confident enough to ask a woman to dance. I always had this fear of rejection. But I did enjoy tapping my toe in time to the music and keeping up the drum beat with my hands and fingers."

"I would dance with you", Diamond sincerely offered. "I'll bet it would be fun to dance with you. You know girls just love a guy who can dance. What about your wife? Doesn't she like to dance?"

"Yes she does, but not the way I like to. I like to glide across the floor, spin her around, dip her and spin her back, but she likes line dancing." Johnny said distastefully as if his style of dancing had class and hers did not.

"Line dancing? Is that country?"

"Oh yes. Texas Two-Step, and Cotton-Eyed Joe. I can't stand country/western music so my wife goes on her own. She takes classes; every Thursday night."

"Aren't you afraid she'll meet someone?"

"No way, she's not the type. She goes out and has a great time, I'm happy for her. She has her hobbies and I have mine."

"Is this one of your hobbies?"

"Oh no, like I said, this is my first time in a place like this."

Johnny rolled the ice in his glass, "I feel kind of guilty taking up your time. I know that while you're talking to me, you're not making any money.

Diamond replied with that shy school girl impersonation, "Are you asking me for a dance?"

"Well yes and no", Johnny hesitated. "I'll pay you for a dance, but I don't want one."

"Oh", said Diamond curiously, "What do you want?"

Johnny looked down at Diamond's foot still dangling, "I just want you to sit here and converse with me a little longer." Johnny took a twenty out of his wallet and handed it to Diamond.

"I'd love to," was Diamond's quick reply. She paused for a moment and gazed into Johnny's eyes as she spoke again slowly, "If you really want me to."

She paused once more as if capturing the moment was a prelude to capturing her prey. She then brushed her hair back with her hand and said, "Besides I cannot leave until I've finished my drink and that usually takes me a couple of songs anyway. Wait until I tell my friend Page about you; she won't believe it. Too bad she's not here tonight; I think she would really like you." Johnny laughed.

Diamond could feel Johnny nibbling the bait; any moment now he would swallow. While continuing to hold Johnny's hand she moved her other arm around his shoulders. She proceeded to massage his neck with her fingers. Johnny responded in the affirmative with a deep breath and exhale while rolling his shoulders back. Johnny closed his eyes and enjoyed the calm he was now experiencing. Diamond began to softly hum in his ear. After a few minutes, Johnny spoke up, "You know, I think I would like to have that dance now."

"Really?" Diamond replied. "I don't want to pressure you. I would love to give you your first dance."

Johnny looked at Diamond a little embarrassed, "Truth be told, I've already had one tonight and I didn't really enjoy it."

Diamond felt the hook was catching, "I tell you hun, until you have had a dance with me, you haven't really had one! I do so want to make your first one memorable. It will be special, just for you. Let's go over to the couch where it can be a little more private and special."

As one song was ending, Diamond stood up and took Johnny by the hand as she led him over to one of the couches on the raised floor behind the stage away from the DJ's speakers. Each couch was in its own private booth with a curtain that could be pulled across it. The sound system was quieter here and Johnny sat down in the middle of the couch. He rested his arms up on the back of the couch. He was totally relaxed. When the next song began, Diamond removed the sheer robe she had been wearing to reveal her sensuous, tanned figure covered minimally with a string bikini.

She leaned forward in front of Johnny with both hands on his shoulders. She nuzzled

Johnny's ear as she moved her long dark hair caressingly along his cheek. She worked her body closer to his as the pulsating beat of the music continued.

Johnny's sense of relaxation was turned to desire. He could not ignore the stimulation he was feeling and felt as though he was suddenly twenty years younger. Diamond would turn about face and lean her back and buttocks against Johnny while moving up and down his torso. Diamond would occasionally let out a soft sound of enjoyable passion which increased Johnny's stimulation and desire for her. Johnny wanted the moment to go on forever, but as the song wound down to completion, so did Diamond. When the music ended, Diamond put one hand on Johnny's shoulder and with the other gently ran her fingers through his hair. She kissed him softly on his cheek and said, "Thanks hun."

"How about one more?" Johnny asked.

Diamond smiled, "My pleasure." She knew Johnny was hooked and she would take her time reeling him in. There would be no fighting from here on out, Johnny was now her catch.

The second dance went much like the first only a little closer and more seductive on Diamond's part. She put Johnny's hands on her waist and removed her top. "It's ok, you can touch me, just be a gentleman." She continued her gyrations on Johnny's lap and repetitive body to body rubbing. Johnny's stimulation was intensifying. He massaged her legs and back in rhythm to the music. He pulled Diamond tightly to him in an embrace and let out several soft moans along with several hip gyrations in sync to hers. He moaned and began to breathe heavier. He pulled Diamond tighter and before the song ended he had ejaculated. When the song finished, Diamond kissed his cheek again and said, "I think you really enjoyed that one."

"I'm sorry, I didn't expect that to happen. I had no idea it would be like this. Diamond, I have to leave now, when can I see you again?"

Diamond smiled, "I'm here every Wednesday, Friday and Saturday hun." Johnny gave her a hug and proceeded to leave. Diamond came out of the booth and looked up at Baby who was dancing on the stage. She gave her a wink while she gestured reeling in a fish.

CHAPTER 4

CORD HAD BEEN THROWING DOLLAR BILLS at Baby's feet on stage as if the well in his wallet would never go dry. As Baby approached him, she went down on one knee and leaned forward for Cord to make another deposit in her bikini top. Cord obliged and worked the bill around her breast and lodged it securely. Baby arose and continued her dance sequence. Cord also stood up, reached into his pocket and tossed up a handful of bills that rained down like the falling leaves of autumn around Baby. As she completed her routine she looked over to her newly found mentor, Diamond, who acknowledged her with a nod and thumbs up.

After Baby had collected her well-deserved rewards she went among her benefactors and thanked each of them individually with a gratuitous kiss on the cheek. The last gentleman she came to was Cord. Her dark almond eyes were beaming. The kiss she placed upon Cord seemed a little more engaging then the others. After which she whispered in his ear, "You like me to spend time with you?"

"I was hoping you could. I didn't know if you already had plans with someone else."

"No, no one else. I want to know you and maybe we have a drink? Give me a few minutes to freshen up. I sticky."

"I'm not going anywhere, take as long as you like." Cord rested his chin on his thumb as his eyes escorted Baby back to the dressing room.

When Baby opened the door to no man's land, she noticed a few girls were also in there changing and taking breaks. They were all discussing the same subjects: they had made little money. They had losers groping them while trying to negotiate lap dance prices. Some even received offers that they did not want to act upon. One dancer commented she had been offered a thousand dollars to meet up at the 'Sleazy 8' after her shift. She told the patron that all she was thinking about after 2:00 a.m. was getting some sleep, not sex.

Another dancer spoke up, "Yeah, there's always the creepy ones. Like that gal that became obsessed with me. A real piece of work. She came in by herself and sat down to the left of the stage drinking a beer. She watched several gals dance but she just sat there as if she wasn't interested. When I went on stage, something sparked. She lit up and started throwing dollar bills at me. She must have showered me with at least thirty. I smiled a lot and gave her some of my best moves. After I freshened up I went back to where she was sitting and thanked her. I asked if she wanted me to stay and talk with her. We had some great conversations and I liked her sense of humor then she asked for a private dance. I gave her three hot ones and she was all over me. I was a bit uncomfortable. I'm open minded you know but the fence doesn't swing both ways for me if you know what I mean. She kept coming back for a few weeks and told me she though we really had something and wanted to take it to the next level, I politely refused. Next thing I know she shows up at my house after shift. I had to get the police involved and get a restraining order. I stayed away from the club for a little over a month. It was a nightmare."

"I hear remember that," said Destiny. "We've all had our share of close calls and ugly nights. There was that one night I thought for a moment I was not going to collect and have to bring in Sweets. I kept asking the jerk if he wanted more and he said yes. After the fifth song he said he was done and I told him that would be a hundred dollars. He freaked out saying that was insane to charge that much for a dance, I told him he had five dances. He said the songs were too short and he didn't realize he was being charged extra. I told him that wasn't my problem. He finally paid me, but he wasn't happy."

Phoenix, who was also in the room primping, spoke up, "That's why I always get the money first!" "Yeah you get the money first but never a second time!" quipped another girl. There was laughter in the room as Phoenix responded, "Oh I get my repeats, but the important thing is I always get my money." The noise and discussions continued as Baby made her way back onto the floor over to Cord.

Cord up stood and extended his hand to Baby as she approached the table. Baby liked his gentlemanly manners. She eyed what he was wearing and how fashionable he looked. His powder blue fitted oxford shirt had darts at the waist drawing attention to his athletic physique. He wasn't wearing a tie. His dark blue designer jeans had probably been steam pressed. He was well groomed and polished with a slight scent of his cologne lingering. Baby liked that. "A clean, handsome man with nice body and nice clothes!" She thought to herself.

Cord's eyes were all over Baby's diminutive frame. She was probably all of five foot-two and sixty percent of her was legs. The three inch wedges that imprisoned her tiny feet were the reasons she could tip the scale at most – one hundred pounds. In Cord's mind he had never seen anyone lovelier. Arousal and desire consumed his being and no sacrifice would be too much to win her affections. Baby graciously accepted Cord's hand and asked, "What your name?"

"Cord." The two sat down together at Cord's booth. "What name are you going by?"

"My name Baby. I don't want to use Hoa Mai."

"That's beautiful. Does it have a special meaning?"

"Yes, morning flower. I never hear anyone name Cord. What it mean?"

"I don't think so", Cord laughed. "You people from different countries and cultures have names that have meaning or significance. Here in America we just have names. Some people have names for a reason; others have the name because their parents had a sense of humor or no common sense whatever."

"What you mean, you people?" Baby said defensively.

"All I mean is people who weren't born in the United States or their parents were from another country."

"And where you think I from?" quizzed Baby.

Cord eyed over her dark skin and small nose. "My guess would be Viet Nam."

Baby was impressed. He was correct. She thought maybe he was just a good guesser. He could have easily said Cambodian or Thai, but he didn't. She realized he meant no offense. Baby thought of her parents and her three siblings still waiting to come to America. Baby shared an apartment with her older sister. They were the oldest, both working, trying to save enough money to bring the rest of the family over. Baby's sister Tran was a waitress at a high end four star restaurant and was taking classes at the local community college preparing for the nursing program. Tran was making good money and Baby was hoping for the same.

Baby had been drifting from several different jobs. She hadn't been that good at clerical or factory work, though she tried hard. She had trouble focusing on the job at hand and paying attention to detail. She worked in a fast food restaurant for a spell but her skin broke out from all the grease she was exposed to. She wanted to work in the Health Care industry but lacked the education. Her plan was to make enough money as an exotic dancer, go to school and bring her family over once she had what she felt was a respectable job.

Baby's parents were traditionally conservative Vietnamese and would not approve of her current occupation. She had hoped she could meet a man who was financially well off who would take care of her. She thought what better place than the Chaise to meet men of means.

Baby looked at Cord and continued, "Maybe you parents name you Cord because you full of energy and electicity."

Cord smiled at her mispronunciation and thought her accent enticing, "That would make a lot of sense; I am a bit of a live wire! I think you have chosen the perfect name: Baby. You are small, frail, and you need to be held and loved. You need a lot of attention and in turn you bring joy to all those who come in contact with you. Yes, Baby. That's the name for you."

Baby gave Cord a bow of admiration. She loved his assessment of her name and its appropriateness. "I hope I bring you joy. You generous," she said. "I don't get much money on stage; it a hope for what can happen later."

"You have brought me much joy already and I look forward to more. I was a little hesitant about coming here tonight." Cord lied, continuing to feed Baby his lines. "This isn't the kind of thing I normally do. But we were celebrating a victory at work and I wanted to stay with the guys. You know, a male bonding kind of thing."

"I understand," said Baby, "Where your friends?" Cord turned around and gave the Chaise the once over. He couldn't see any of the guys. He looked again and again and noticed that there weren't as many patrons as when they first arrived. He realized it was getting late and he had been so caught up in watching Baby on and off the stage that he hadn't noticed them leaving. "I guess they're gone," he said.

"That ok", said Baby, "We don't want interruption."

"I don't see how anyone could." Cord's eyes were fixed intensely upon Baby's. He put his thumb and index finger under Baby's chin as he lifted her face closer to his. "From the moment I saw you tonight, I knew I had to meet you. I wanted to be near you. Not because you are beautiful, but because you looked real. So many of the girls in here look fake and act fake. But there was just something genuine about you and I had to know more. Maybe it was your dark alluring eyes that captivated me or maybe just your soft warm smile,"

Baby loved the way Cord spoke to her. Though she had some trouble understanding Cord when he was talking, she was sure he was saying beautiful things to hear. He was not like the few gentleman Baby had entertained in her short tenure at the Chaise. She liked him. His words were like a song to her. She just wanted to hum while he spoke. She provided Cord with this reasoning, "Maybe it because I'm new. I just try to be myself. I don't know how to be anyone else."

"Please don't ever be anything or anyone else," added Cord. "You are perfect now, don't change a thing. Can I buy you a drink?"

"Sure," said Baby, "Bottled water."

"Are you kidding me? You don't want any alcohol?" Cord questioned.

"I would like some green tea, but they not have it here. I need to bring from home." Baby again giggled.

"Then you shall have it, and I shall have a dance or two, unless of course you are too tired."

"Never too tired to dance. I love to dance. We wait for next song." Baby then pointed to the private booths. "We get drinks then go over there."

A waitress came by with Baby's bottled water and another cocktail for Cord. The waitress smiled and added a sweet thank you for the five Cord gave her for her tip. Baby took a few swallows of her water, smiled and escorted Cord to an empty couch. As it was approaching 1:00 in the morning, the private dances were as few as patrons in the club. When a new song started, Baby took control. She moved her long black hair back and forth across Cord's face and chest. Her perfume was intoxicating. It was a subtle scent that complimented her like spring blossoms on a cherry tree.

She unbuttoned two buttons on his shirt and kissed his chest. Baby took it slow, no fast movements and no jerking gyrations.

Everything was smooth and sensual. She sat on his lap and tossed her head back on Cord's shoulder. He couldn't resist, he kissed her on the neck. Baby was surprised but didn't pull back. She enjoyed it. She was feeling the same kind of stimulation that Cord was. She turned and faced him. She put her arms around him and pulled him closer to her own body. Cord obliged and put his arms around her and held her tight. He couldn't believe the softness of her skin. She was as soft as the dawn's light on Manhattan Beach. She put her head on his shoulder and pulled her hair back. She then kissed Cord softly on his neck. Cord was no longer holding Baby. He was massaging her back and sides. He was so caught up in her soft skin he nearly forgot not only who he was but where he was.

The music was perfect, slow and sultry. The beat was light and subtle, not pounding like so many of the other songs. Cord was leaning back in the couch enjoying all the attention Baby was giving him. He leisurely drew her close to him, looked into her eyes and kissed her lips. Baby did not pull away, she reciprocated.

The music began to fade as another song segued. Baby pulled back and said, "What happened? Where that come from? Why I let you do that? That not allowed. I could get fired!" She paused and spoke slower trying to be more articulate, "I wanted that and you knew. That scare me!"

Cord straightened up, "I know, I've never done anything like that before. Please forgive me. I don't know what came over me. I felt like I was in a dream and it seemed the natural thing to do. I won't do that again. Maybe it was the booze? All I know is I want to be able to come in here and see you again. I promise I'll behave. I'll control myself."

Baby looked at Cord not knowing what to say. The problem was she did want him to kiss her and that should not have been the case, at least not in the Chaise. "It alright," Baby said. "Come in and see me again, and behave yourself, or I call Sweets."

"Sweets?" asked Cord.

Baby pointed to the powerfully built figure with his arms folded in the corner just past the stage.

Cord said he needed to be getting home and handed Baby the cash for the dance along with a tip. She quietly buried the money in her modest pocket book. Cord said goodnight and delicately held her hand while putting his arm around her. Baby began to think, "Could this be the well-to-do man who might have affection for me and take me out of this place?" She couldn't remember if she saw a ring on his finger or not. All she knew was she had an attraction to him and she liked it when he kissed her.

CHAPTER 5

WHEN JOE LEFT THE CHAISE, HE had no plans of immediately heading home. It was Friday night. The night was still young and he could get out of bed whenever he wanted to tomorrow since it was Saturday. He got into his silver Accord and headed towards the seedier streets the LA area had to offer.

Joe was heading toward the Garment District. All the stores were closed. The long blocks stretched out in the darkness. The streetlights did little to identify what the shadows were hiding in the alley. Joe was on the hunt. He was trolling for a lady of the evening who for the right price could scratch his itch.

The streets were pretty much deserted and the prospects were slim in this area of town. The girls working here were fewer and cheaper than those found on the Sunset Strip or Hollywood Boulevard. If there were any working girls out, they would be the bargain basement brand.

All the stores were enclosed with iron bar fronts. Graffiti was the contemporary décor on all the buildings. Joe drove up and down one street after another. It was as though he was cruising a ghost town. The homeless gathered to their designated spots huddling together for warmth and settling in for the night. Once the sun had gone down, the heat that had covered downtown earlier was nothing more than a fading memory disappearing in the moonlight. Joe was preparing to turn around and head home when he caught a glimpse of a potential target.

She stood close to five-foot seven in black leather boots that came up to her knees. Her black spandex skirt exposed about six inches of thigh. She wore a faux fur jacket that was tight and stopped at her waist. Her frame was lean and the clothes she wore would most likely have come from an adult store. Her hair was tousled and combed with her fingers. Her makeup was light and she fit in well with the evening shadows.

She was exactly what Joe was looking for. Not too pretty which was fine with him. The pretty ones were usually bait for a sting and there had been a few as of late. The last thing Joe needed was to get "John'd". Joe knew if they were on the pretty, they were high priced.

Joe was always a little nervous and uncomfortable of the approach and making the first move. It wasn't something he did on a regular basis. He was paranoid and distrusting. Still he had that craving that needed to be satisfied. He pulled his car over to the right up against the curb and when he caught her attention, he rolled down the window and asked, "What's up?"

"What's up with you?" She replied.

"I'm just cruising about hoping to find some action." She came closer to the car and leaned on the window frame.

"Looking for a nightcap? You're not a cop are you?" She whispered.

"No, I'm just a guy who needs a little something, you know." Joe smiled.

"Well how much you talking hun?"

"I was thinking $100."

"That's not enough, I never go less than $150." She said with pride.

"Come on, I've only got $100. Besides it's late and wouldn't it be better to take home a hundred rather than nothing at all? Besides, I'm quick."

"Ok, I'll do you for $100. But like you say, it's gotta be quick."

"You have a place? I don't have money for a motel and I didn't see any close by. I guess there's always the car."

"I don't do cars. I have a place. Just pull over here and park. It's around the corner. It's better for us to walk since there's no parking over there. It's jus a couple of minutes from here."

Joe pulled his car up a little further and parked. He met her on the sidewalk and she took his arm and pulled him closer to her. His anxiety was wearing off. Joe was sure he scored. The two of them started their walk down the block.

"Do you date often?" She inquired.

"No, but sometimes I just need it, you know?"

"Oh I know baby. What's your name?"

"Joe"

"Joe, really? I've know a lot of Joes, but a lot more Johns." She grinned.

"Yes, I really am a Joe. What's yours?"

"Well I don't really have a name but you can call me Esther. You know, from the Bible."

"From the Bible, that surprises me."

"Yes, I've always admired Esther, such an incredible and brave woman. I only wish I were more like her. Do not think that because of what I'm doing I'm not religious. You don't mind if I hum or whistle do you?"

"No, I guess not."

Esther began to hum what sounded like a hymn to Joe but he didn't know for sure since he wasn't a church goer himself. He enjoyed the tune and as they approached the corner she began to whistle. This was certainly louder than her hum but Joe thought nothing of it. As they approached the corner, Joe became uneasy as he heard someone else whistling. As they turned the corner a large man stood face to face with them.

"Let's have the money." He demanded

Joe knew he was in trouble. He hadn't counted on a pimp. "We were still negotiating. I only have forty dollars."

"What kind of crap are you trying to pull?" The pimp bellowed ferociously.

"Really, that's all I got." Joe said.

The pimp looked over at Esther in anger.

"He told me $100, honest." Esther's voice was quivering.

The pimp looked at Joe and cold cocked him. Joe never saw it coming, his knees buckled and his head hit the concrete. Joe was only out for a few seconds and began moaning. The pimp took Joe's wallet and pulled out an ATM card. "What's the pin"

"No way." Whispered Joe. "Besides I have already maxed the limit today."

The pimp began to kick Joe in the ribs with a violent force. "I'm not going to ask you again, what's the pin?" This time he got down on Joe and put his knee in the middle of Joe's back and with both hands began to pull his head back. "Tell me now or I'll break your neck."

Joe unable to move said, "6161."

"Thanks, you've just paid for your date." The pimp stomped the heel of his steel toed boot onto Joe's fingers. Joe let out another cry as he heard the bones in his fingers crack. The pimp then looked over at Esther, "Get his keys, we're going for a ride." With that, Esther and her pimp took off in Joe's car with his ATM card, leaving him semi-conscious and bleeding on the sidewalk.

CHAPTER 6

I T WAS WELL PAST MIDNIGHT WHEN Johnny finally made it home. He was fortunate that he had only three drinks at the Chaise and spent enough time there that his driving would not be impaired. He was tired as he struggled to find the keyhole and unlock the door. He was thankful Jenny was her usual considerate self and left the light on. He let himself in and made his way to the bedroom. As he prepared himself for bed, he noticed how peacefully Jenny was sleeping. He knew her day with the boys had been long. He also knew she wouldn't trade it for anything. He thought of what a devoted mother and dutiful wife she was. He felt guilty and ashamed of his actions at the Chaise but at the same time recognized the void it filled and how he enjoyed it. He slipped silently into bed without disturbing Jenny. His thoughts continued to dwell on the Chaise and Diamond until he drifted off into a deep sleep.

Johnny awoke to the smell of freshly cooked bacon. Jenny was already busy in the kitchen. She loved preparing Saturday breakfast. Pancakes were done and warming in the oven. The hash browns were a crisp golden brown flavored with diced onions. The aroma of freshly brewed coffee was a delightful scent. The table was already set with a pitcher of orange juice from the refrigerator. Johnny walked into the kitchen tying off his robe. He smiled at Jenny as if to speak, but Jenny spoke first, "How do you want your eggs? Johnny put in his order,

"I'll have two eggs over easy if you please."

"Two over easy coming right up." Jenny was amused with her short order cook reply.

Johnny was pleased. He felt like a king and he loved being catered to.

"Well bring your plate over here; the food isn't going to get there on its own!"

Johnny brought his plate to Jenny. She scooped out a hearty portion of the hash browns and laid them on his plate. She pulled three pancakes out of the oven and said, "They haven't been buttered yet, you'll need to do that."

Johnny picked out a couple of pieces of bacon while Jenny slid his eggs out of the pan onto his plate. He poured himself a cup of coffee and sat down at the table. Then Jenny started to scramble some eggs for herself. She liked her eggs well done and dry. She knew Johnny would break his yokes and let them run into his hash browns. He loved soaking them up. Jenny thought that was disgusting and almost like eating a raw egg.

Jenny put her plate together with scrambled eggs and hash browns. She then poured herself a glass of orange juice. She was not a coffee drinker like Johnny. She didn't mind coffee with her dessert or after dinner, but that was about it. Johnny on the other hand could be seen with a coffee mug in his right hand at any given time of the day when he was at work. He was not the continuous coffee drinker at home like he was at work. Still he was known for an occasional cup while in the house relaxing; especially at Saturday breakfast.

Jenny sat down at the table with Johnny. She bowed her head and silently blessed her food. With her blessing said, she picked up the newspaper.

"Do you want any part of the paper?"

"No, I don't think so," Johnny replied. "I do not need to read about prima donnas whose 15 million a year for playing a game they loved to play as a kid just isn't enough. Or politicians in scandals or the world coming to an end. I don't want anything to interrupt the delicious breakfast I am devouring.

Jenny started folding the comic section; she looked up at Johnny and asked, "I'm sorry, what did you say?"

Johnny took another swallow of his coffee and replied, "No, thanks; I'm fine."

The two sat quietly at the table while eating their breakfast. Jenny took her time with the paper. There were several articles she would read word for word and others would get a paragraph or two. Sometimes a headline would catch her eye and she would quickly glean through the first paragraph in order to decide if it was worth her time to read more.

In hopes of starting a conversation, Johnny would ask her what was new in the world. Jenny would then recap an abridged version of what she had read. Sometimes she would hand Johnny a section and tell him he could read for himself.

Johnny couldn't understand why he and Jenny had little to talk about. He wondered why he had no trouble talking about a variety of different subjects with his peers at work and they all engaged in the conversation together. He also wondered why it had been so easy for him to talk to Diamond at the Chaise last night and tell her things he had not told anyone else. He pondered why he had been able to talk with a stranger for more than two hours and feel like they had only scratched the surface and yet have nothing to discuss with his companion? He couldn't believe that after 35 years he and Jenny had nothing more to talk about.

"What time are you guys going to the zoo?" Johnny asked, hoping to stimulate some dialogue.

"Eleven O' clock", Jenny replied. "And it's not the zoo, it's a petting zoo. They are different you know. A petting zoo is small farm animals like goats and sheep that the kids can go in an pet. And there's also rabbits and chickens for them to feed with pellets and meal that they can purchase there."

"I get it." Johnny sighed. "But you know how I am. On some things I don't get into the details. You know I call any soda a Coke no matter what it is."

Jenny knew Johnny wasn't getting defensive nor was she trying to be antagonistic.

"So, Jim, Maddy and the kids will be coming here then?" Johnny asked.

"No, Jim has to work. It will be just Maddy, me and the boys today. I thought I would take them all out for a nice lunch afterward."

"Sounds like a great idea," said Johnny in agreement. "Is there anything I need to do for you today?"

"No, I don't think so. Just enjoy your day today. What are your plans?" Jenny picked up her glass and finished her orange juice.

"I thought I'd attack the lawns; they're looking pretty shaggy. It's already 9:30 and the weather looks cooperative today; a little bit cooler than yesterday but the afternoon will still be hot. After that, I'll clean up and listen to those new CDs I picked up. I've been so busy with this last project at work that I haven't taken time for anything else. It will be nice to unwind." Johnny wiped a napkin across his mouth and left the table with his coffee cup in hand.

Jenny picked up Johnny's dishes along with hers, went into the kitchen and commenced cleaning up the morning's meal. She hummed to herself as she rinsed off the plates and stacked them up for a later wash. She put away the food still on the counter. After wiping down the counter, Jenny got out celery, apples, raisins, bread and some cookies and spread them over the counter. Johnny eyed the activity in the kitchen and asked, "What are you making?"

"I'm putting together snacks for our adventure."

"What are you going to do with all that bread? How many sandwiches are you making?" said Johnny looking confused.

"Some of it is for the ducks. The boys will love feeding them."

"Ah, that makes sense. I'm going to put on some clothes and hit the lawns before the day gets away from me. I don't want to bake out there," Johnny smiled and went towards the bedroom. Jenny continued her work in the kitchen.

A few minutes before eleven, Maddy pulled up the driveway with her boys. David and Jonathan leaped out of the car and charged up to the porch.

"Grandma, grandma, we're here," as they burst through the front door in excitement. Jenny braced herself while they surrounded her, embracing her legs.

"Boys, let grandma in the house," Maddy sighed as she spoke. "They've been up since seven and have been asking if it's time to go every thirty minutes."

"Well I'm glad they're excited," Jenny said, "We're going to have a fun adventure today." Jenny bent down and put her arms around both boys and kissed them. As she stood up, the boys took off for the back room where Jenny kept their toys.

David and Jonathan were boys in every sense of the word. They had endless energy and were always inventing new pretend adventures to keep themselves amused. The two years age difference didn't seem to matter. They were the best of friends.

They loved to wrestle with each other. This activity was always performed in the back yard when at Johnny's house. Johnny would not allow rough housing indoors. He did however play ball with the boys outside and taught them to catch and throw a baseball as well as dribble a basketball. He put up a small backboard and hoop so the boys could shoot baskets. It was just the right height for them. Johnny was all too aware of how an eight year old and a six year old could destroy thirty-five years of accumulated treasures in ten minutes. Johnny loved the boys but he was intolerant of his peace and serenity being disturbed. It also bothered him to no end to see toys and games scattered all over. He never complained, he would stew a little in silence and then retreat to his office – the one room in the house where the boys were not allowed.

Johnny came in from the back yard into the kitchen looking hot and dusty; beads of sweat were welling up on his forehead. He filled a glass with water from the sink and satisfied his thirst. The boys saw Johnny in the kitchen and waved to him. When he finished, he put the glass down and walked over to the boys and tussled their hair.

"We're going on an adventure today," David blurted out. He could hardly contain his excitement while he was bouncing up and down.

"Are you coming Grandpa?" asked Jonathan.

"No son, Grandpa has some work he wants to get done today. But you have fun with your mom and grandma."

"We will," David responded, "Daddy has to work today so he can't come," Jonathan added.

Jenny and Maddy came into the kitchen and the boys quickly rushed over to them. Jenny started to gather up the snacks, treats and peanut butter and jelly sandwiches and put them in the boys' backpacks. She then picked up the container with the relish cuts and apples.

"It looks like you're all set," mentioned Johnny as he passed by Jenny. "Where is this place anyway?"

"It's just up a little bit off the 210 at a place called Granger's Farm. It takes a little over an hour to get there. OK everyone, let's get moving." Jenny motioned to the boys and they picked up their backpacks. Jenny and Maddy made their way to the car while Johnny saw them to the door. "Have a great time everyone," he said as he waved good-bye.

Jenny and Maddy would talk the entire drive. The two of them had so much to share. Nothing could please Jenny more than to see Maddy raising her children the same way she had raised Maddy. Maddy had married young, but that didn't seem to bother Jenny. She was content that Maddy had done all she wanted to do as a single young woman and felt she was ready for marriage and a family. She felt that Maddy's marriage to Jim was the crowning achievement to her motherhood. Maddy was a registered nurse.

Before she and Johnny were married Jenny had just been accepted into the college nursing program. Jenny was always in the school library studying. Johnny had already graduated in accounting and was finishing up his MBA. When they first met Johnny mistook her for the part time help and asked where he could find the latest issue of the Harvard Business Review. Jenny wasn't sure if she should feel complimented or insulted.

"I have no idea," she politely replied.

Johnny looked puzzled for a moment and said, "You don't work here do you?"

"No," she said.

They had a little laugh and Johnny apologized. Over the next two weeks Johnny would purposely run into Jenny at the library and break up her intense studying to quietly engage in small talk for a few minutes. Johnny had never felt at ease with the opposite sex and after three weeks finally asked Jenny if she would like to go out with him. To which Jenny replied, "Of course I would; what took you so long?"

Johnny and Jenny had dated for a year. Johnny was finished with school and was working as a financial analyst for an engineering firm. Theirs was not a storybook romance by any stretch of the imagination. They were in love, but not in a lovesick romantic sort of way. They were more like partners, not starry eyed lovers. Johnny never formally proposed. He suggested it was probably time they get married. It came off as more of a proposition for a business merger. They were quietly married by a local minister with a few friends and family.

Jenny became pregnant within two months of the marriage and dropped out of school due to the difficult nature of her pregnancy. Her obstetrician was concerned about the development of the baby and recommended terminating the fetus. Jenny refused. She was sure in her own mind that everything would be alright and that she was supposed to have this baby.

At the time of delivery there were complications. The baby was out of position and a c-section was performed. The baby was fine but Jenny was hemorrhaging. The doctors performed emergency surgery on Jenny. Her life was spared, but her days of bearing children were over.

Jenny's physical recovery went quick. The doctors were impressed with how well she had healed. Her emotional recovery took much longer. Johnny did everything he could to console her although his efforts for the most part were in vain. While Jenny was convalescing, she told Johnny she did not want to go back to school. She was content to be a mother and a wife. Johnny said he was making enough money and was aware of Jenny's sensitive emotional nature. He agreed it best for her to become a stay at home mom. He was sure that in time Jenny would go back to school and complete her dream of becoming a nurse. Jenny stayed home, totally devoted to Maddy and never went back to school and never regretted it.

When Maddy pulled up to Granger's farm, the boys were asleep in the back seat. Jenny looked back at her two little angels, calling their names and letting them know they had arrived. As Maddy opened the car doors the boys sprang to life. They could see cows, goats and sheep. They grabbed their back packs and bounced out of the car. It truly was an adventure for them.

After they ate their sandwiches, they went and fed the chickens that were out in a pen pecking at the ground in hopes of finding food. The boys loved watching them run to whomever they thought had the grain. They were allowed to pet sheep, feed a lamb with a bottle and toss bread to the ducks in the pond. There were also geese at the pond but the boys steered clear of them as per their mother's instruction. The high point of the day was the boys getting to ride a pony.

Each boy was dressed up like a cowboy and put on a pony that was escorted around in a circle in the corral. Jenny's heart was full watching the boys having so much fun as well as seeing how much Maddy loved them.

On the way home, they stopped off at Miss Molly's Diner for dinner. The diner was known for its 50's – 60's rock & roll atmosphere. Their menu was full of novelty specialties such as the James Dean 'Hot Rod Hot Dog' and the 'Elvis Club'. Desserts included 'Shake, Rattle and Roll' milkshakes and Four Seasons 'Cherry Pie'.

Jenny thought Johnny might love this place with all the posters and memorabilia of the great music she loved. She knew Johnny's taste in music differed from hers, but thought he might appreciate the nostalgic setting. Jenny thought about what a nice date that would make for the two of them some night. She felt disheartened by the fact that they just seemed so busy all the time and could never get their free time in sync with each other.

CHAPTER 7

WHEN JENNY ARRIVED BACK AT THE house, it was already close to 7:30. Johnny had been relaxing in his office listening to his new CDs. He heard Jenny opening the door and came out to greet her. She had backpacks in her hands and asked Johnny to bring in the cooler. Johnny asked for a summary of the day's events. Jenny told him everything in detail including the geese giving Jonathan the evil eye. She then showed Johnny the pictures of the little cowboys on their ponies. Jenny told Johnny about Miss Molly's Diner and how much he would have loved it and that they needed to go there someday.

Johnny enjoyed how animated Jenny was describing the outing. He loved to see her happy and knew how much she loved spending time with Maddy and the boys.

Johnny spoke up, "What do say we go the deli, get a pastrami and hit a movie?"

Jenny replied, "You haven't eaten yet?"

"No," said Johnny, "I was waiting for you."

Jenny sighed and shook her head, "Well that's really sweet of you, but I'm still stuffed from the diner. They give you a lot of food. I'm also pretty drained from everything we did today. I was hoping just to sit back and unwind the rest of the night. I think you should go. I'll be fine here. I don't think I would be good company anyway as tired as I am."

Johnny put his hands on Jenny's shoulders and massaged them gently "Alright he said, I'll be thinking of you while I'm putting down a Reuben."

Johnny was amused with himself for he knew his Jenny could not stand the smell of sauerkraut let alone eat it! Johnny continued, "As for the movie, I was thinking of a chick flick, but since it's just me, I'll find something with a high body count and a lot of destruction. Anything you want me to do before I go out?"

"No I'm sure there isn't anything that can't wait until later. Besides, I am going to early church tomorrow and want a good night's sleep." And with that said, Jenny walked into the kitchen and began to unload what was left in the backpacks and cooler. "You did my dishes, what a sweetheart." Jenny smiled and turned to look back at Johnny but he was already in the bedroom.

Johnny went to the closet to get a sport coat even though it was still warm out. His attire was casual, which for Johnny meant khaki style slacks and a polo shirt with the top button unbuttoned. Johnny carried his coat out to his car and drove off to the deli. As much as Johnny loved a good Reuben, he did not go out to eat often. He was completely content with whatever Jenny would fix.

Johnny was pretty frugal even though he carried a large amount of cash on his person. He would have as much as five-hundred dollars at times. He wanted to make sure that if there was a circumstance where he would need the money, he was prepared. He always had a soft spot for the homeless and panhandlers and thought nothing of giving a twenty dollar bill when they put the bite on him.

Occasionally he would take Jenny out for a sandwich or a nice dinner. He knew how hard she worked around the house every day and realized her days were always full and he wanted to give her some relief from what he saw as a mundane life. What he didn't realize was Jenny never saw it that way. She was completely content and very happy with her life as a wife and mother.

Once inside the deli, Johnny was told it would be a few minutes before a booth would be available. He was given the option of sitting at the counter; but Johnny liked the privacy and comfort of a booth. The wait was short and Johnny didn't care. He figured as long as he was paying for it, he should get what he wanted and not have to compromise in order to save a few minutes. Besides he wasn't in any hurry.

After ordering his Reuben, potato salad and a soda, Johnny thought about the current movie selection and what he might enjoy. There were computer animated films which were popular with many. Johnny did not enjoy them because he felt there was too much innuendo in what was supposedly a children's movie and he thought most of the scripts were too corny.

There were some romance and adventure films, but they did not seem to fit the bill for what Johnny was in the mood for. In fact Johnny was not sure what exactly he had in mind as far as seeing a movie by himself.

The waitress brought over Johnny's order and said, "Here you go hun, enjoy." The waitress's comment brought back the sound of Diamond's voice. It was as though he could hear her summoning him. His mind was made up. He would go to the Chaise. Diamond said she would be there on Wednesdays, Fridays and Saturdays. What a perfect opportunity. Jenny had already given him permission to go out tonight. Not that he felt he needed her consent. Still it was nice to know that it was her idea that he should go out.

Johnny took his time with his meal. Although anticipation was building up inside, he wasn't about to let the deli patrons see it. He didn't want anything to look out of the ordinary. He was a cautious man. Johnny even ordered his usual dessert, apple pie ala mode. Upon finishing his meal, Johnny left a twenty dollar bill on the table and headed for the door.

"Thanks hun; see you soon." Johnny turned and waved a goodnight gesture and walked out to his car.

As Johnny scanned the Chaise parking lot, it became apparent to him it would be another capacity crowd. After all it was past nine o'clock on a Saturday night and the evening's guests had already arrived in force. Johnny didn't mind parking his Mustang in a less discretionary quarter of the lot as he did the previous night. In order to conceal his anticipation Johnny walked at a regular pace up to the Chaise and stood in front of the velvet curtains. Another large well-built man patted Johnny down and said, "Enjoy yourself."

Sweets stood off near the bar adjacent to the DJ's den with his arms folded at his chest. He was stalwart and secure. Confident that as long he stood firm, there would be no trouble. And that pretty much was the case. There were exceptions of course when a gentleman would get a bit out of line whether it be due to the vast consumption of alcohol or possibly just a lack of good manners. It didn't seem to matter to Sweets; he just did his job and took care of business.

The most memorable disturbance was during a bachelor party at the Chaise. The best man got it into his head that he was a better stripper than the ones he was laying his bills down for and he decided to prove it. He got up on the the stage where one of the girls was dancing and proceeded to do his own pole dance and striptease.

By the time Sweets pushed through the cackling crowd, the gentleman was down to his tighty-whities and only athletic socks still on.

Sweets carried him off the stage in wedgie style and hurled him and three of his friends out the door. He then tossed out all personal belongings residing in the gentleman's pants pockets to the parking lot. Sweets kept the discarded pants as a souvenir for himself. He later framed them and hung them on one of the walls above the Men's Room with the following inscription, "Don't disrespect the girls." This served as a notice to all patrons there would be consequences if they thought they could get away with stiffing the dancers. It was also a reminder that inappropriate behavior would not be tolerated.

The Chaise ladies were in fine form. Their lipstick was fresh and wet, their eyes widened with mascara and shadow and there was the subtle scent of their perfume which could be breathed in for those who were lucky enough to get cheek to cheek. Their lingerie was accented with stiletto heels ready to meet the stage and potential private shows.

The air was alive with fantasies and dreams which would be lived out in a few hours. Here a man could always look desirable to the woman he so envisioned to be his goddess and trophy, provided he still had money. For here at the Chaise, even the loneliest and least enviable of men could have his ego stroked and his wallet lightened. As long as the wallets were full and the laps were warm, no man had any call to be alone.

Page, Diamond's roommate who was working that night, was in the dressing room having a latte before starting her shift. Baby and Phoenix were already on the floor with the other girls eyeing the unsuspecting victims of the Chaise savannah. It was Saturday night and there was plentiful bounty to be had.

Phoenix quickly eyed any newcomers or gentleman she didn't recognize. She was keenly aware that repeat business was not her forte although that didn't stop her from trying. She kept watch for the opportunity that would allow her to strike quickly upon the unsuspecting and take advantage of those less educated in the ways of the Chaise.

At the Chase, Diamond was just checking in. She went into the dressing room and found Page. She went over to her locker and Page sat beside her. "We haven't had a chance to talk, but I wanted to let you know about this guy that came in last night." Page listened intently as she twirled her bobbed hair beneath her ear.

"Oh you would love this guy. His name is Johnny and he is the perfect dupe! I knew right away he was kind and naïve and I could tell he was lonely and frustrated. And boy was I right!"

Diamond's assessment was correct. Johnny was a newcomer just looking for something, but had no idea what. Most importantly, Diamond had managed to have Johnny let down his shield and bring her into his world and he would pay to keep her there.

"He sounds like a great guy," Page commented as she sipped more of her customized brew.

"Oh he is. And guys like him are the easiest to take as you know. And the best part is, they never know you are taking them."

Page nodded and pushed her hair back from her eyes, "I do not know how you always find them but you do. Well, I've had a few like that myself. Enjoy it while you can, the money won't last long."

Diamond smiled back at Page with great pride in her voice, "That is for sure. God knows I've been doing it long enough. I know how to play the game."

Diamond applied some perfume on her wrist and rubbed her two wrists together. The dressing room door opened and Baby came in stammering, "You no believe this. He is here!"

"Who's here?" Diamond looked puzzled.

"You Johnny. He back!"

"What, Johnny from last night?"

Baby nodded.

"Well," said Diamond as she stood up and flipped her auburn locks into place with a shake. "This is an unexpected surprise." Diamond's eye's lighted up like headlights at dusk. "This guy not only took the bait, sounds like he swallowed the hook." There was laughter in Diamond's voice as she spoke. "You girls pay attention now. You want to know how to play the game? Just keep your eye on me and you'll learn. Oh I am so loving this. I was pretty sure he'd be back but not this soon! Baby, where is he sitting?"

"About three booths from center stage." Baby pointed him out through the slightly opened door.

Diamond looked in the mirror one more time at her lipstick, she pulled her lips back and examined her teeth for any unsightly residue. She walked toward the dressing room door and turned to her companions as she opened it, "OK girls, it's show time!"

Johnny sat uneasy in his seat as he scanned the Chaise for Diamond. He had already finished one beer and couldn't believe she was nowhere to be found. He was sure he hadn't misunderstood her when she told him she would be here tonight. His mind continued to wander; "Maybe she's on break or called in sick." Then one thought came to him which was disturbing, maybe she lied.

Johnny's insecure nature took off like a sprinter. It all made sense now. Why would an attractive woman like her see anything in a boring old man such as himself? He told himself that this was a bad idea and it was wrong for him to be here. He didn't belong in a place like this. Suddenly, guilt began to set in.

He didn't notice Diamond walking in front of him heading towards the back stage. As she came near the stage, Johnny finally detected her. He tried to make eye contact but Diamond was looking down at the floor rather than straight ahead. Johnny could tell something was bothering her.

He didn't call out her name because he didn't want to call attention to himself. Johnny's heart was pounding. She was here after all. Now if he could only get her attention before she moved on or before someone else requested her company. She stopped for a moment and said something to one of the Chaise girls and then shook her head. She turned in Johnny's direction momentarily and then turned away before Johnny could catch her eye. As the song came to a close she applauded the girl on stage. She turned once more and headed back in Johnny's direction. Johnny was not about to let her get by him a second time. He stood up and sheepishly waved his hand and said, "Hello."

Diamond looked at Johnny as if she had just awoken from a trance. "Well hi hun, I didn't see you there. What a nice surprise. I didn't expect to see you again so soon." She paused for a moment. "How was your day? Are you enjoying yourself tonight, there's plenty of beautiful girls here to entertain you and keep you company."

Johnny was a little bit taken back by Diamond's response. He was hoping for a little more enthusiasm from her, but then again he was only with her a short time last night and possibly the connection he felt was one-sided.

"It's been an ok Saturday; I got some yard work done, listened to some new music, read for a while, had dinner and now I'm here. I'm here because, well I was hoping to see you and spend a little more time with you. I'm not really interested in any of the other girls. In fact I almost left when I thought you weren't here."

"You're so sweet," she said as she patted his hand. "I'm afraid I won't be good company tonight."

"Why not?" Johnny stepped into the snare as he asked, "What's wrong? You look depressed."

"Thanks for your concern hun, but it's my problem and I need to deal with it." Diamond took hold of Johnny's hands in hers, looked at him directly and said, "Besides, there's nothing you can do about it."

"Well maybe I can't, but I can listen."

"Thanks hun, I don't want to sound rude but the last thing I need is sympathy." Diamond's voice was agitated and callous as she let go of Johnny's hands. Believe me, there's nothing you can do for me." Diamond stood up as if to walk away. Johnny put his hand on her arm.

"Wait, please have a drink with me, I meant no offense."

"OK hun, sure. I need a drink. Maybe I need a lot of drinks." Her tone was now sarcastic. "Like I told you, I'm not good company tonight."

Johnny flagged the waitress holding up his empty beer bottle, "Tanqueray on the rocks with a cranberry chaser for the lady here and I'll have another beer." The waitress nodded in acknowledgement and went off to the bar.

Diamond put her arm around Johnny and rubbed his shoulder. "How sweet of you to remember. I didn't mean to be short with you, but it seems like everything is crashing on me at once. I don't know what I'm going do." Her voice was more relaxed and soft.

Johnny played the part of the concerned knight giving Diamond's hand a squeeze and said, "Now tell me about your troubles."

Diamond felt the snare tightening up. Johnny had stepped in with both feet and was now her quarry. Her eyes, full of warmth and sincerity met Johnny's as she toyed with him.

"I don't know where to begin. I guess it all started with my car problems two weeks ago. It's an old clunker and gets me around just fine but it would just stop all of a sudden for no reason when it had been running just fine. It didn't matter if it was on the street or the freeway. It could have been running for ten minutes or over an hour. It didn't matter. Then, when I finally got it to start again it would backfire like a bomb. I got it to a friend of mine who's a mechanic and he worked on it for a few days. He didn't go much into details and I am not that familiar with cars, I think it was the distribution."

"The distributor'" Johnny corrected. "I'm no mechanic, but I am familiar with the individual parts."

"Yeah, that's it. Well anyway, things have been really slow here at the Chaise, at least for me, and I needed to take care of my registration. I've been expired for over a month, but with my rent, the car problems and one of the girls ripped me off here last week and..."

"What?" Johnny's face displayed his disbelief.

"Yeah who'd've thought? A few of us have been ripped off over the last several months. We have no idea who's doing it.

"Why don't they put cameras in the dressing room?"

"Are you kidding? They have cameras everywhere in this place. We girls want at least one place where we can go to that's private besides the toilet. Anyway, so I've finally got my car running again and I was planning on getting the registration taken care of next week.

"Now get this, I'm driving back from the grocery store when this cop stops me. He first tries to put on the charm and be nice and then starts asking me a bunch of personal questions and suggest maybe we should go out for lunch and stuff like that. I ask him to tell me the problem and get on with it. He tells me I have expired plates and he's going to call it in. Now he starts acting like a real jerk and then he tells me I have several outstanding parking tickets on my car and he's going to take it in. So he tows away my car and leaves me stranded out there on Central with just my groceries."

"Unbelievable!" Johnny sat there shaking his head.

"I was fortunate that Page, my roommate, who is also here tonight, was home and picked me up. She's kind of been my taxi lately but she can't take me everywhere and now with fines, towing and late fees my registration is going to cost three hundred dollars. And the rent fee for my car at the yard is twenty dollars a day! I don't see that I'll have the cash until sometime next week because it's rent time again. By the time I'm flush, another week will have gone by and that raises the price up another hundred and forty bucks! So there you have it, my money miseries."

Diamond was near tears by this time. Her wide eyes were glassy and wet. Her voice was cracking. Johnny now saw Diamond in a different light. She was more than a sex object that danced and removed her clothes for money. She was an individual, an individual just like him. A being that once detached out of this world of erotic fantasy, had a reality. A harsh one, but a reality none the less.

Johnny thought of his own reality, his wife, his job, his predictable routine and boring life. Johnny had been taken in by Diamond's dilemma. He wanted to do something about her reality since she provided him with an escape from his. The waitress arrived with the drinks. Before she could ask for the money, Johnny handed her thirty dollars as if routine and said, "Thanks."

Although Johnny had been known for being prudent when it came to money, he understood how things worked at the Chaise after his previous night's excursion and came prepared to indulge in all the benefits.

Johnny took a long swallow of his beer. He was quiet and deep in thought. He hesitated as he began to speak, "Diamond, you're in a predicament. You've got a serious problem and it needs to be solved immediately. You don't have the means to solve this problem right now; I do. Let me help you. I solve problems for a living; I can solve this one."

Diamond looked at Johnny as though she couldn't believe what she was hearing.

"No Johnny, I can't let you, why would you? You don't know me. I'll find a way, I'll get Page to help, or something."

Johnny reached into his pocket, retrieved his money clip and brought forth six fifty dollar bills. He thought of himself as a playboy philanthropist even though that was hardly the case. But here at the Chaise he could be anyone he wanted to be and he didn't what to be Johnny Bradford, typical boring, middle-aged husband. He truly felt like a man now. He was a hero in Diamond's eyes. Johnny imagined the two of them riding off into the sunset on his golden palomino with her on his lap. Then he thought again, "Sheesh, how cliché."

"Here, take it, I probably would have spent it here at some point. I'd rather see you take it and put it to some good. You're right, I don't know you, but what I do know is that you gave me something I really needed last night and now I'm returning the favor."

Diamond draped her arms around Jonny's neck and kissed him softly on the cheek. "Oh Johnny, you're an angel. I'll pay you back, I swear."

Johnny secured his arms around Diamond's waist and held her close to him. As they were cheek to cheek he whispered, "Forget it. Just let me hold you like this for a few drinks."

"We can do that," she said as she kissed his neck. Diamond sat on Johnny's lap as he held her tightly in his arms. Diamond kept her arms loosely around his neck and shoulders. She had been watching the activity at the bar and whispered in Johnny's ear, "Watch out, I believe there's going to be trouble."

Johnny turned his head towards the bar where Diamond was looking and could see what appeared to be an allocation between a male patron and two of the dancers. There was a lot of finger pointing between the dancers and the patron. One of the dancers began to shout at the client and slapped him. The other dancer threw her drink in the face of the one dancer, punched her in the face and grabbed her by the hair. The both fell off the bar stools and began to roll on the floor punching, screaming and kicking at each other.

"Oh my gosh, a cat fight, it's Venus and Summer" Diamond said snickering. Before she could say anything else, Sweets and another bouncer came and broke it up. Sweets grabbed Venus, the dancer on top of the other, by the back of her neck and lifted her off the floor with one hand and carried her to the dressing room. The other bouncer picked Summer up off the floor and wiped her face with a towel while walking her to the opposite end of the Chaise. Within minutes Sweets came out of the dressing room holding Venus tightly by the right arm while she wheeled her roller bag. Sweets escorted her out of the Chaise to her car. He came back through the velvet curtains and walked up to summer. "Get your things, you're out of here."

Diamond could fell the anxiety and tenseness within Johnny. She smiled at him and said, "Just another crazy night at the Chaise." Johnny was frozen. He couldn't believe what he had just witnessed. He wondered what kind of situation he had walked into. He didn't know what to make of it all. "Is it like this often?"

"Not at all hun. But that was something huh? Buy Sweets sure took care of that in a hurry."

"I thought for a moment there would be a raid and police would be called in."

"Nonsense. Sweets always has things under control. Besides there are always a couple of off duty cops in here if we need them."

"Does this sort of thing happen often?"

"No, but is does add a little excitement don't you think?

"To be honest, I was scared, I didn't know what to think."

"I can tell you what this was all about if you like."

"You know what's going on?"

"Sure the guy at the bar is a semi regular, Leroy. Leroy has spent time with a number of girls in here but mostly with Venus and Summer. They don't usually work the same night. Leroy has been sleeping with the both of them and how they didn't figure it out until now is beyond me. He's a real loser and why they would fight over him is beyond me. You may not have noticed but a soon as the fighting started, Leroy snuck out of here and took off for the hills." Diamond brought her hand to her mouth as she laughed.

"Well, I think I've had about enough for one night. I'll see you soon. Take care of yourself."

"I always do Johnny, and thanks again for coming to me in my hour of need.

CHAPTER 8

T HE MIDDAY SUN PEERED ITS WAY through the blinds thin slats onto the navy silk sleep mask Diamond wore. Her roommate Page came into the bedroom and shook Diamond's uncovered ankle and sat herself down.

"It's after 2:30. When are you planning on getting up?"

A muffled voice returned, "As soon as I can smell coffee. Be a dear and bring me a Bloody Mary." Diamond had more than her usual last night thanks to a few gentlemen seeing that she didn't want for thirst. She was in hangover hell.

Diamond sat up on the bed and pushed her sleep mask to the top of her head. Most of her makeup had been washed away before turning in. There were still smudges over her cheeks and her eyes had faint circles under them. Her lips were pale and her hair was mussed in different directions. In twelve hours she gained ten years.

Page came back with the transfusion Diamond requested. Diamond took the glass from Page and began to sip her morning medication and take deep breathes as if coming out of a long coma. Page lit up a cigarette and asked, "So, how did you and your man make out last night? I notice he didn't stay long and you didn't even get a dance out of him."

"You're right, I didn't get a dance out of him; just $300."

"Go on, you're kidding, right?"

"Nope, he felt sorry for me and my troubles and gave me $300 to get my car fixed and out of tow."

"There is nothing wrong with your car; and it's not in tow!"

"I know that and you know that, but he doesn't. As far as he knows, you are my transportation and when he sees me again I'll thank him for getting me my car back. All he wanted to do was sit there and comfort me. I love it."

"Wow, you are incredible. So what's next?"

"I'm not sure. I don't know how far he is willing to go just yet. He seems to be a lonely guy who just wants a little companionship. I doubt that he is looking for anything else. When I did dance for him, the night before, he was nervous. He wasn't sure if he should touch me or not. When I told him it was ok, he began to softly rub me; not grope and grab like most of the guys. It was as if he thought of me as his girlfriend for those three and a half minutes. And then he really got into it and shot his wad. Oh, by the way, there was a cat fight last night."

"What? You're kidding?"

Nope, Leroy got caught with his hands in two cookie jars, Venus and Summer's. It didn't last long and Sweets took care of things quickly. It was fun to watch while it lasted. Scared the crap out of Johnny. I had to calm him down. He'll be alright and he'll be back.

Page switched her crossed legs and exhaled the recycled smoke. She pushed her bangs away with one hand while her other hand held her cigarette.

"I had one like Johnny. Kind of shy, cautious. Everything seemed just like you said. Cool and reserved the first dance, respectful the second, but by the time we got to the fifth dance his hands were everywhere, and I mean everywhere. I couldn't keep up with him. After the fifth I said, I have to get ready to go on stage. He paid me, thanked me, and we were done."

"I'm telling you Page, Johnny is different. He is not the kind to keep going once he gets a little taste to see just how much he can get. I think he is content just to have me pay attention to him. I'm going to take him slow. I believe the well goes deep here and I am going to get all I can before I let him go."

"What if he doesn't go? What if he hangs on and won't go?"

"They all go sooner or later. There comes a time when they all recognize it's a game and they have played long enough. Johnny will too. I'm hoping he just takes longer than most. What time are you going in?"

"I am going in at 4:00. Just a short shift; I bet I will be done by 10:00. Sundays are usually quiet. I am hoping to make cover and come out with $200."

"OK, I'm going to freshen up, have my coffee and see if there is any action in town."

"You be careful girl. The cops have been cracking down lately. I heard three girls got busted over a week ago. You watch yourself."

"Things should be fine. Now that they've had a bust, I expect the streets to have settled down. Of course, most guys are a little reluctant to come out after a bust, but I'll check it out just the same."

When Diamond left her apartment to go on the prowl she was once again transformed. Her auburn hair graced her bare shoulders. She wore a grey knit tube top. Her black spandex skirt covered just enough of her thighs while leaving the unexposed a mystery. Her makeup was light and mostly hidden by the large sunglasses which served as more of a mask than a shield to diminish the sunshine's glare.

Diamond walked in a steady rhythm towards the Café Bistro, a local favorite of hers for a number of years. The restaurant was close to downtown with outdoor seating. Upon arriving, she took an outside table with an umbrella. She ordered her usual latte with a slice of cheesecake. From where she sat, she could eye all who came and went. When eyeing the potential prospects, she would give a slight nod of the head followed with a smile that suggested, "Looking for something?" But for all her preparations and patience, nothing came her way.

Diamond signaled to her waiter, "I'll have another latte." As he took Diamond's order, a voice called out. "I'll take care of that." She looked up to see Ron Crocker standing at her table.

"Well look what the cat drug in? How long has it been Ron?"

"A couple of months anyway. I've been pretty busy at work.

Diamond sipped on her latte, "I guess so; I haven't even seen you at the club."

"Was there just two nights ago. The place was pretty packed. I didn't notice you there."

"Oh, I must have been busy. Like you say it was pretty packed. And were you entertained?"

"Most definitely. Our boss Johnny from work showed up. He'd never been in a strip club before. You should have seen him. He was so totally lost. We bought him a dance and he was practically humiliated. We all laughed about it afterwards. He's a great guy and he knew we were just trying to get him to loosen up. No harm done. I am sure he's seen enough."

Diamond was taken back when she had heard Johnny's name. She couldn't believe he was Ron's boss. She laughed to herself at the irony of it all. "This is going to make things interesting if not complicated," she thought to herself. "So did you just stop by to buy me another cup or do you have something else on your mind?"

"Well I didn't when I was walking around out here. Especially since I read about the sting a few nights back. But when I saw you, I thought it might be nice to renew our friendship. Unless of course you are otherwise occupied or have something scheduled."

"No, I'm available. I would like to finish my latte and cheesecake, if that is alright."

"Take your time. I've got nothing else going on. Besides, it is a beautiful day out and I'm enjoying the sun as well as the scenery."

Diamond took another bite of her cheesecake. "You are such a charmer. Almost as sweet as this." She pointed her fork to the last bite of her cheesecake, "But not quite."

"Yes, they do make a great cheesecake here. Same arrangements as before for an old friend? I am hoping the price hasn't gone up."

"No it hasn't. Two hundred for my time, a room at the Embassy and dinner this evening."

Ron, reached into his wallet and pulled out a twenty and laid it on the table. "Fair enough," he said as he stood up and walked over to Diamond. She held out her hand and said with a smile, "Let us be off."

Ron escorted Diamond from her table to the parking lot where his car would take the two of them to the Embassy Hotel.

CHAPTER 9

P AGE ARRIVED AT THE CHAISE A little before four in the afternoon. It was the usual Sunday, quiet. Six hungry felines preying upon ten potential victims who were content to sit at the bar and enjoy the Sunday discounts while watching a sporting event on the big screen above the bar. Occasionally they observed the eye candy on stage and would throw a gratuitous dollar or two to appease them.

By seven o'clock, Page had downed her fair share of vodka tonics and managed to pull in several dances from some of her regulars. Most of it went to the house but she was thankful she had made cover.

Page walked over to Baby who was alone in a booth fingering her cell phone. "How about you, getting much action?"

"Too slow, need more men. I get some, but not enough." Baby never looked up. She was engrossed with her cell phone rather than conversation.

"Who are you texting girl? Possible hook-up?" Page smiled and raised her eyebrows.

"No, some nice guy I met here."

"That's risky, no one saw you give out your number did they? Management does not like that."

"No, I careful. He come back soon. Sends me sweet texts."

"Well you better be careful, I don't trust any of the guys who come in here. You can't believe any of them"

"Oh not Cord, he different."

"Yeah, aren't they all?" Replied Page sarcastically.

The sunset was approaching in the Los Angeles area and the temperature was cooling. The summer days had been in the high 80's with little relief in sight. As the evening progressed, a curious figure made his way through the velvet gateway. He was elderly. He looked to be in his seventies. He was overdressed for both the club and the weather. His dark sharkskin suit was tailored and fit him sound. He was lean in build and approximately five foot ten, although in his prime he may have been six foot. He wasn't hunched and didn't stoop although he walked slowly with a cane he tightly grasped in his right hand.

A black fedora with a red feather on the side hid his snowy white hair. As he emerged from the curtains and sauntered past the bar, he held a small package in his left hand that he waved high above his head to the ladies in the club. It was a pair of fishnet stockings.

"It's Mister Freaky," Page whispered to Baby.

"Who Mister Freaky?"

"Mr. Freaky shows up occasionally and has peculiar needs. He comes in waving his package of fishnets around while looking over all the girls. Then he picks one to attend to him. He gives her the stockings and tells her to change. When she comes back, they go to a private room for a while."

"What he like?"

"Well, we call him Mr. Freaky for a reason. After getting dressed in the fishnets he brought we go to a room. He has us dance a little bit facing him and massaging his cheeks. He moans a little and then says "Give it to me." At that point we move our hands from his cheeks and begin to choke him. Not hard enough to strangle mind you, but enough so it's erotic for him. Now comes the crazy part."

"You mean that not crazy!"

"No. Now he says, "I want it." We start kicking him in the nuts. He says "Yes" and "Oh yeah" several times until he's almost completely out of breath. I went in with him once and thought he was going to die on me. He gave me a $200 tip and let me keep the stockings so what the hell!"

"I could not do that, scare me to death"

"I hear ya, the things we do for money." Page laughed.

"Some things I not do."

"He's still searching, oh I think he's found who he wants. Looks like Destiny, good for her, she can use the money. I have no doubt she will be able to take care of Mr. Freaky"

Mr. Freaky smiled and raised his eyebrows to Destiny. He then beckoned his head towards the private rooms and winked. Destiny smiled, walked over to him and took the stockings out of his hand. "Be right back, don't go anywhere, I won't be long," the enchantress seductively crooned.

Page grinned back at Baby, "Well when you have a kid, you do what you have to do."

"What? She have a child? What she doing here?" Baby looked confused as she spoke. She couldn't believe a mother would be at the Chaise instead of home tending to her child. "What kind of mother could do that," she thought.

"She's doing what we all do hun, paying the bills. She has her boy every other week; this is her off week, so she works here. It pays better than waiting tables."

"Yes, I know. My sister works in restaurant and I make more than her. Destiny not look like she have baby, her body in good shape."

"Destiny looks good alight, but she's had four years to work it off. If you get close to her, you can tell; stretch marks don't lie. Besides, she's not the only one, a few of girls here have kids. Just because we are strippers doesn't mean we aren't vulnerable to the seemingly irresistible male charms. I'm bored, I think I'll get another drink"

Page went and sat at the bar with Phoenix. She pondered if it was worth staying for another hour. There were probably thirty prospects in the club now and she had already made her move on most of them. There was one well built, athletic looking man in his twenties, sitting in a booth with a group of guys the same age. He was attractive, and seemed to be controlling all the conversation while laughter occasionally emerged from the group. Page asked Phoenix, "Who is that guy? You ever see him before?"

Phoenix smirked, "You really don't know who that is? Where have you been?"

"I don't know. I've never noticed him."

"Well, if you ask him, he'll tell you he's God's gift, but if you ask me, he's more of a white elephant."

"What do you mean? He looks ok to me."

"That's Trevor Johnson, the all-star college quarterback and complete asshole that's expected to be the number one pick in the draft. He's arrogant and thinks he's entitled if you know what I mean. I had once dance with him and that was enough."

"Yeah, for you it usually is. I'm going to see if I can make a few more bucks before I leave. Wish me luck."

"You're going need it." Phoenix shook her head as Page walked over to Trevor and his group.

Page put her hand on Trevor's shoulder and remarked, "Wow, you're pretty firm, care for some company?"

"Pretty firm, are you kidding he's rock hard!" replied one of Trevor's friends from the group.

"Don't you know who this is?" replied another, "He's Trevor Johnson!"

"No I don't know who he is and I couldn't care less about his Johnson!" Page laughed.

"Sounds like we need a dance so you can learn all about me." Trevor replied.

"OK, what will we talk about during the second half of the song?" Page had the entire group laughing.

Trevor stood up and took Page by the hand, "Let's go over to the booths."

Page led Trevor over to the booth area behind the couches. The booth area was shielded behind another set of velvet curtains similar to the entrance. In the booth area there were two rows of five stalls against the walls each with a padded leather bench for the customer to sit on. The stalls were a tight fit, but there was enough room for the dancers to perform for their clients. The area was lit with soft red lights.

Page picked a corner booth and Trevor sat on the bench. She kicked off her heels and put her hands on Trevor's shoulders and leaned forward to him as the music started. She moved rhythmically to the pulsating music while rubbing her cheek against his then turning with her back towards him and shaking her lower torso. She sat down on his lap gyrating erotically while tossing her head back on his shoulder and softly moaning. Trevor's hands were moving all across her body as Page continued to turn and establish a new position in the booth when she felt his hands were wandering where they shouldn't. As the song ended and segued into another pounding stream, Page whispered, "Would you like more?"

"Of course I want more. Give it to me."

Page started her routine again, only this time a little differently. She undid the scarf that hung from her shoulders in crisscross fashion and kept her breast supported to reveal a little more of what was hidden beneath.

Trevor was now a bobble-head following her every move. With every sway and turn Pge would divulge a little more of what was concealed. As the song was ending and another queued up, Page once again asked, "Would you like more?"

"Absolutely."

Page now pulled out all the stops. She removed her scarf and pulled down her spandex skirt with only a black thong remaining. Trevor's eyes scanned every inch of her now exposed body. His mind went wild with excitement wondering what could possibly be next and where would this lead. He felt soon there would be another notch of conquest on his already loaded gun.

When the song ended, Page said, "I hope you enjoyed it." Trevor straighten his shoulders and sat upright and spoke, "You have no idea."

"Actually, I have. And do you have something for me?"

"Oh do I," as he grabbed his crotch, "but I'm going to give you some cash right now," he smiled as he handed her $30.

"Page looked at the ten and twenty he gave her and replied, "You owe me a little more. That was three songs."

"No that was one long song; no way was that three!" he argued.

Page quickly put herself back together and pressed a button on the outside of the booth. Within seconds a hulking, concerned Sweets looked at Page and asked, "Is there a problem?"

"Yes, he won't pay me for all the dances."

Sweets frowned at Trevor and in his deep commanding voice asked, "Is that true?"

"No, it was just one long dance, I don't know where she comes up with this three crap!"

Page looked up at Sweets, "Now Sweets, after each dance I asked him if he wanted more and he said yes."

Sweets questioned Trevor again, "Did she ask you if you wanted more?"

"Yes, but I though she meant she was going to show me more. I couldn't tell that the song ended, they all sound the same."

Sweets held up a finger and pointed at Trevor's chest, "I know when you went in there and I know when you were done. It was three songs, you owe her $90."

"Well I don't have it, what are you going do?" shouted Trevor.

Sweets put his huge hand on the back on Trevor's necked and squeezed.

Trevor winced and began yelling expletives at Sweets. Sweets marched him out of the booth and up to the front counter. He pointed to two gentleman not far from the stage and signaled for them to come over. When they came to the front desk, Sweets said, "We may have a problem here. This gentleman doesn't way to pay for the special attention he was given in the booth." Sweets looked eye to eye with Trevor and said, "These boys here are two of LA's finest and see to it that the air of dignity and honesty at the Chaise is upheld." Sweets looked over at the plain clothes officers. "I believe he even propositioned our sweet Page here."

One of the officers spoke up, "That's a criminal offense. I'd hate to take you in with the draft coming up. Yes I know who you are. Sweets is there some way we can work this out without ruining my night by generating a lot of paperwork?"

Sweets said, "I have a solution." He looked at Trevor and asked, "Do you have a credit card?"

"Yes. Why?"

"Give me your credit card and I'll make this right. Then we'll forget this unfortunate incident ever occurred."

Trevor hesitantly pulled a credit card out of his wallet and gave it to Sweets. Sweets looked it over and swiped it on the register. A receipt came out and Sweets handed the receipt and a pen to Trevor.

"This is for $150! This is outrageous. I'm not signing it."

"Yes you are," fired back Sweets, "Unless you want to go home with these boys. Just so you know, you left Page a nice tip for the exceptional entertainment she provided."

Trevor signed the receipt and then brought up a clenched fist toward Sweets but backed downed almost immediately once Sweets faced up to him, chest to chest.

"You haven't seen the last of me," yelled Trevor as he stormed through the velvet curtains into the parking lot.

"Oh yes we have," replied Sweets, "And if we see your sorry ass in here again, you're going downtown."

"That bitch is going to pay," he thought as he walked to his late model corvette.

Sweets handed Page her cash. "Thanks, you are the best. I'm going to change and head home. I've had enough entertainment for one night."

CHAPTER 10

———————●

A NOTHER MONDAY AT RAYCOM. BY 8:00 am the air permeated with the aroma of freshly brewed coffee. While keyboards clicked, discussions could be heard re-enacting the weekend's sporting events. Johnny was already at his desk reviewing his calendar. There were a number of meetings he needed to attend and a few he did not want to. Through the open door, Ron Crocker peered his head in and asked, "Got a minute?"

"Sure Ron, come on in. What's on your mind?"

"Joe won't be in today."

"Hmmm, too bad, is he sick?"

Ron walked over to Johnny's office door and closed it. He walked back to Johnny's desk and sat down in one of the office chairs. He leaned over the desk and spoke softly to Johnny."Joe got rolled Friday."

"What are you talking about? Rolled?"

Ron nodded. "The fool went out looking for action in the Garment district after midnight. He was…"

Johnny interrupted, "You mean a prostitute?"

"Yeah, he went looking for a whore. He was in the wrong place at the wrong time. I got a call from him around 12:45 am. He could hardly talk and said he had been mugged and his car stolen. When he told me where he was, I kind of put two and two together. When I found him, he was a mess. He really got the hell beat out of him. I took him to the ER, filled out some paperwork and left him there."

"Good heavens, poor guy."

"What are you talking about? He had no business down there at that time of night. He was just asking for trouble. I don't know why he just didn't go to the Desert Rose Spa earlier if he needed it that bad."

"Desert Rose Spa? What's that?"

"You have never seen it? It's a massage parlor off Figueroa in a strip mall. I'm sure Miss Lee would treat him right." Ron winked.

"You sound like you are pretty familiar with their operation. So if I were to show up I could say Ron sent me?"

"Well I don't know about that, I'm not sure if they even know a Ron."

Johnny looked surprised. "Ron, I've known you a long time and in the past few days I'm learning all kinds of new things about you. I had no idea what a cynic you are when it comes to women and the low opinion you have towards them. I often wondered why you had never married. I mean you're good-looking as far as guys go, have a great job and you are really a nice guy."

"Funny you should bring that up. There was this gal. There is always a woman, isn't there. Her name was Lorraine. She was attractive, not that it mattered, and I was in love. We went everywhere and did everything together, restaurants, shows, clubs, you name it. I spent everything I had on her.

I was still in college when we first met and I drove this beat up old Chevy. She was kind of embarrassed to be seen in it, but she went with me just the same. She complained I didn't dress sharp enough and I needed to update my wardrobe. I would have liked to do that, but I was spending more money on her than myself. It didn't matter though, I loved her. Of course I wasn't the only guy she was seeing at the time. I did not mind because she would always come back when things went sour with the others. We had been together about two years when I asked her to marry me. She turned me down. She said she wasn't ready to live in poverty and support me through school. That was the last I saw of her. She did call me a few times. She hooked up with this real estate broker who was making good money, but he soon grew tired of the good times with her and decided he needed to spend more time with his wife and kids. After that she developed a taste for coke. She even called me asking for money. That's when I hung up on her and got a new phone. I've had a few other relationships, but none of them panned out."

"Come on Ron, there are plenty of good women out there. Women who would be wonderful wives and caring mothers to your children. Most important of all, you two would share your love and life together."

"You should not bring up love. Love! Do not believe the lie. Love is a pain in the ass. There is no weapon in the world that can destroy a man faster than love. Anyway, easy for you to say, you got yours, and what a treasure Jen is."

Johnny lowered his head for a moment and pondered Ron's comment. Just like Ron, everyone saw Jenny as a treasure and viewed Johnny as one of the luckiest guys around. He thought Jenny was a great wife and mother, but something was missing. He felt she never loved him the way he wanted to be loved. He started to feel guilty about his thoughts of Diamond and saw himself as a hypocrite. "You're right, she is a treasure."

"Anyway, that's not what I came to talk to you about. The big boss wants to see you."

"You mean Big Al? Why does he want to see me?"

"He probably wants to give you congrats and kudos on CCMT."

"Oh good, as long as I am not in trouble."

Al Rogers was vice president of operations at RayCom. He had been in the business over 20 years and was an excellent salesman and negotiator. He was a down to earth manager as well. He was just as comfortable walking the factory floor, and talking to employees as he was in the board rooms making executive decisions.

Everyone knew him as Big Al. He didn't seem to mind. He was tall and a bit overweight. He loved a good meal and liked to drink. He was personable and easy to talk to.

Johnny walked up to his office and knocked on the open door. Al got up from his chair and walked over to Johnny. "Come in Johnny," he said and shook his hand. "Well done on the CCMT project. Great work. Nobody else wanted it and many thought it an impossible task. But you took it on and developed a team that delivered. The stake holders were impressed and you are getting the right kind of visibility."

"Thanks boss, I appreciate that."

"So Johnny, as I have said, your work has not gone unnoticed. In fact the executive committee has decided you are the best man for another project. I assume you have heard of the prototype for the X-Lab project."

"Sure I have. You can just follow the trail of former managers and employees whose failure to deliver has left it behind schedule and over budget. It is a plague that everyone in their right mind stays clear of."

"Johnny, the committee wants you to take it over. I believe you are the only one who can deliver."

"You mean I am the only one left in the company that has not been part of the collateral damage. I do not want it. I'm getting close to retirement and I would not want this red mark on my resume when I go out."

"Nonsense. You know how to approach things differently. This needs a new set of eyes. There is a lot of money riding on this contract. This is RayCom's future. And just between you and me, the leader who runs this project and delivers will be the next Director of Operations. A great fit for you with a nice pay increase and bonus perks. That would be a nice way to go out on your retirement, wouldn't it?"

"Do I have a choice in this matter?"

"Not really. The decision has already been made, but I wanted to present it to you like this so you could feel it was your decision, not theirs."

"Can I pick my own team?"

"Bring on whomever you want."

"What's the schedule for the prototype?"

"Delivery is scheduled for 4 months from today."

"Thanks boss, I guess I better get started." Johnny stood up and headed for the door. Al followed him and shook his hand once more.

"I know you will deliver Johnny. We are all counting on you. I know you are the best man for the job. Thanks for taking this on. I will send out a memo later today and make it official." Johnny headed back towards his office wondering if he had just picked up the gauntlet of doom.

After lunch Johnny assembled a group of employees in a conference room. Ron Crocker, Paul Miller, and Cord Williams were among those in attendance. The scuttlebutt and rumors had been going around the water cooler for a couple of hours ever since Johnny announced a mandatory meeting. There was talk of a re-org and also Johnny's possible retirement. Johnny stood up and said, "Let's get started. I know you are all wondering what this is all about. Well it is all about the great work you have recently done. Because of that, we have been being given a new opportunity. I will get to the point. I have been chosen to lead the prototype for the X-Lab project and I have chosen all of you to be on the team. I hope you will all join me in this opportunity."

Johnny was not expecting applause and cheering. He was however stunned by the silence. He could see the disappointment and uncertainty in all their faces.

"Come on folks, say something. This is a good thing." Johnny continued to scan the eyes of discontent around the room. Finally, Paul Miller spoke up. "You are kidding, right? That project is a pariah. All of those previously involved were fired. You might as well have booked us on the Titanic!"

Ron Crocker stood up and faced the group. "You're right Paul, even though your analysis is not. The previous teams were unsuccessful. Well there are lessons to be learned from that." "We will not follow the same processes. We will not build on the derivative technology. We will establish a new set of rules for change management and configuration control. Look around. Johnny has once again assembled the best project engineers, architects, security experts, developers and project managers in the company. If we cannot build this, nobody can."

Confidence in the room began to swell. Cord Williams stood up and applauded. The applause became contagious as one by one the employees stood up in solidarity clapping. Last of all, Paul Miller stood up and put his hands together.

"Ok", said Johnny as he stood back up. "Now that everyone is on board, we need to develop a plan. I will see that everyone has all the documentation that is associated with this. Ron will be your technical lead. I leave you all in his good hands.

Johnny left the conference room and walked back to his office. He was beginning to feel better about the project, although he had other thoughts on his mind now. He wondered how he was going to survive until Wednesday when he would see Diamond again.

CHAPTER 11

BY WEDNESDAY JOE MADE HIS WAY back to work. He resembled a prizefighter having gone ten rounds with the champ and losing. The left side of his face was badly bruised and his cheek was swollen. His right arm was in a sling with his fingers splinted and mounted on a round plastic support that resembled a child's catcher's mitt. Joe limped over to his cubicle and with his one good hand began setting things up for the day. Johnny noticed him walking the floor and went up to his cubicle.

"Joe, can you come into my office for a quick chat?" Joe nodded and met Johnny in the aisle as they slowly walked towards Johnny's office. Once they were in his office, Johnny closed his door and sat behind his desk while Joe sat off to the side.

"Well Joe, I understand you ran into a bit of trouble last Friday." Johnny's tone was sympathetic and full of concern. "I want you to know I feel for you. That is not the kind of experience I would want to go through. I am glad you are all right. How are you feeling?

"I won't lie Johnny. I am sore and embarrassed. I am sure the folks are talking. I am not sure how I can face them."

"You can face them Joe. Right now, Ron and I are the only ones who know the exact details of your unfortunate incident. And that's the way it is going to remain. As far as anyone is concerned you were the victim of a mugging and carjacking. If anyone asks, tell them you do not want to go into details and the police are handling the matter. You can also tell them that you are thankful things were not worse and you just want to heal and have things get back to normal again."

"Thanks for understanding Johnny. That means a lot. I am done with that kind of activity. It was stupid and you are right, I am probably lucky to be alive."

"Speaking of work, I have got some good news for you. I have chosen you to be a part of the team I have assembled for a challenging project. Keep in mind, the greater the challenge, the greater the prize."

"Awesome Johnny, what project?'

"X-Lab".

There was an uneasy look about Joe's face. He wanted to scowl but the swelling made it difficult. His left arm on Johnny's desk held his head in one hand as he added his doubt. "You cannot be serious. That prototype cannot be built with our current resources and tools. When is delivery?"

"Less than four months. Joe, you are one of the sharpest configuration management trouble-shooters in the industry, when you want to be. I know you can make this happen. I need you. We can do this."

"Sure Johnny, remember what you said about things could be worse? You were right. I will support you and do all I can. Get me the specs as soon as you can. We will find a way." Joe stood up and hobbled towards the door shaking his head and muttering to himself.

Johnny stood up out of his chair. "Like you said, we will find a way." Joe made his way out of the office while Johnny remained steadfast and confident about the project and team.

Joe was working his way back to his cubicle when he passed by Dana Pulley whose goal in life was spreading the dirt in other people's lives in order to make her life look better. Dana Pulley, or Dangerous Dana as she was known in some circles due to her two victorious sexual harassment suits, was another malcontent. She had been involved in a few of Johnny's projects but was never comfortable with his recommendations or decisions.

Dana always felt she had a better idea. Many of her own implementations and designs violated best practices and company standards to such an extreme they were borderline unethical. She could also be belligerent at times if decisions did not go her way. Despite her attitude and behavior, she was a sharp and competent programmer. She did not acknowledge anyone as her peer since she esteemed herself in a much higher light.

She distrusted management. In her mind, they were incompetent and biased. She was exceedingly paranoid. She would complete her assigned tasks utilizing her own methodologies which no one else seemed to understand. This made support difficult and gave Dana the impression she was indispensable. As far as reliability was concerned, Dana took advantage of the very generous sick leave policy at RayCom at least twice a month.

Dana looked at Joe and asked, "What the hell happened to you? I heard you were sick. What gives?"

Joe was uneasy talking to Dana about his mugging knowing Dana the way he did. But he answered her just the same. "I was car jacked Friday night. I was just cruising, heading back home around midnight when this gal runs into the street and starts waving her hands to get me to stop. I pull over and roll down the window to talk to her and the next thing I know is there is this big dude with a gun in my face telling me to get out of the car."

"Oh my God." Dana looked at Joe in shock as he continued.

"I did as he told me, you know I did not want any trouble. As I am getting out of the car, he punches me in the face with the gun in his hand. I fall to the street and he begins kicking me."

Dana looked puzzled. "Why didn't he just get into the car and drive off?"

"I have no idea. Finally he stomps on my hand and then he and the girl drive off."

"How horrible. Did you file a police report? How did you get home?"

"Fortunately I still had my cell. I called Ron and he took me to the hospital. I filed a police report there. They haven't found my car and I imagine it probably has a new owner somewhere in Mexico now."

"How awful. Good thing you didn't resist; that maniac might have shot you. Well it is good to have you back. Have you heard the news?"

"You mean the X-Lab project? Johnny just gave me the bad news."

Dana reached over and patted Joe's left hand as if he were her lap dog and needed some reassurance. "The news isn't as bad as everyone thinks. I have been doing some research and it appears to me that the issues lie within the product data manager or PDM. I think it has some compatibility problems with the configuration management software we are using."

"Well everyone says the product data is inaccurate."

"I know a developer at one of our suppliers that works on this type of application. I think together we might be able to resolve this problem. We could sure use your help on this. If we resolve this, we will all be heroes. Are you with me Joe?"

Joe thought about the proposition. He now saw Dana in a different light and he liked what he saw. This could be his chance for the promotion that kept eluding him year after year. He pondered whether or not he still had the skill to deep dive into a source code he was unfamiliar with and resolve the issues. He was taken aback by the fact that suddenly he was attracted to Dana, something he had never given a second thought to in the past because of her reputation. He sensed two enticing opportunities here.

"I'm waiting, what do you think?" Dana was getting anxious and was a little disturbed that Joe had seemed to lose focus. Joe smiled at Dana and said, "I'm in."

CHAPTER 12

CORD HAD BEEN MAKING HIS WAY back to the Chaise on Sundays. It had been three weeks since he had met Baby. He hadn't missed a Sunday since he first saw her after the Friday night celebration at Portello's. He was fascinated with her. He was consumed with lust and desire and wanted her more than anything, if only for a little while.

He wasn't spending the kind of money Johnny was but he was spending enough. He would get between 3 or 4 lap dances from Baby, share a drink and be gone. He didn't want to stay out too long since he was a family man. He would make excuses to his wife about attending a sports bar to watch an event with the boys.

Although Cord was smitten with Baby, he was the one in control. He was a charmer and a smooth talker. He had Baby in the palm of his hand and he knew it. He would tell her things like, "I've never met anyone like you." Or "I can't believe how lucky I am to have found you. You're the one I've always been looking for." Baby was easy prey for his cheap sentiment and insincere flattery. She was young and naïve. She enjoyed Cord's compliments and he had a way of speaking to her as if she were in a romance novel.

The second time they were together at the Chaise, Cord convinced her that they should share phone numbers so Cord could text her with his feelings for her whenever he was thinking about her. Baby saw no harm in this and obliged. Cord would send between three and four texts a day at different times. He always sent a text just before going to bed telling her how much he wished she was with him. Baby ate it all up.

Cord would do most of his texting with Baby during his working hours at RayCom. On this afternoon his text began with the following welcome:

"Hey Morning Flower, are you in bloom?"

"Yes, I am awake." was Baby's reply.

Cord typed back, "How are you feeling? Was last night a good night for you?"

"No, slow, not much money." She added a sad faced emoji.

"Well things are slow for me as well here at work. I thought it would be nice to come by and see you."

"At my apartment?"

"Sure, why not? Your sister is at school isn't she? I can break away. I really want to see you."

"What would we do? My apartment is small."

"We don't have to do anything. I just want to look at you and hold you. I would also like to share this bottle of wine with you. I am sure it would bring a smile to that beautiful face of yours. I would only stay about an hour."

"That sound nice. When you come?"

"Well I'm downtown right now. Where do you live?"

"I live close to Chaise. I send you address."

After Baby sent her address Cord typed back, "See you in about 30 minutes" and added a heart emoji.

Cord left the office and began driving through the city streets of LA. He didn't need to get on the freeway and he was glad since the homeward commute for many was just getting started. Baby's apartment was about 10 miles away and traffic was moving at a good pace. Cord was correct in his estimate. He was at Baby's apartment within 30 minutes.

The apartment complex was old and in need of attention. The grey stucco was peeling in a number of areas and the landscaping was all but forgotten. The hoary edifice housed somewhere in the neighborhood of 200 units and parking was inside the complex for tenants only.

Cord found an open parking lot about a block away from the apartment complex. The parking was $10. Cord slid two five dollar bills through the metal slot that corresponded to the number on his parking space. He got the bottle of wine out of the car and proceeded towards the worn-out structure. It had minimal security and Cord had to dial Baby's number to be buzzed inside. Once inside the building he ascended the three flights of stairs to Baby's apartment.

He knocked on the door. Through a small opening of the apartment door appeared two almond eyes. The door opened with Baby scooting behind it as Cord came in. Cord's eyes opened with excitement when he looked upon Baby. She was dressed in a short green silk kimono robe that draped down to the tops of her thighs. She was bare-legged and the rubber flip-flops on her petite feet exposed toes whose polish had been neglected. Her face was clean of makeup from the previous night.

Cord looked into her eyes and gave her a hug. He liked the way her body felt in the silk robe. "You are beautiful. It doesn't matter what time of day or night or where you are, you are beautiful."

Baby bowed her head and said, "You sweet."

Cord handed her the wine. "Take this and get a couple of glasses."

"OK, but I not big drinker." Baby came back with two wine glasses each half full. She handed one to Cord who held his up and said, "A toast, a toast to the good times we share and the memories engraved upon our hearts." Cord clinked his glass with Baby's. Baby took a sip and then looked up to Cord, "I love hear you talk. Your words like a song."

"It's nice in here," Cord said. "Let's go sit down." He put his arm around Baby and brought her towards the couch. Baby sat down in the center of the couch and crossed her right leg over left. Cord sat down at the right end with his left arm still around Baby and the wine glass in his right hand. Cord couldn't get over how sexy she looked and how much he wanted her.

"This is more like it. Are you comfortable?"

"Yes, I comfortable."

"Great; you like the wine?"

"Yes, it good."

"Good, I'm glad you like it." Cord pulled Baby closer to himself. He brought his face close to Baby's and asked, "Are you happy?"

"Yes, I happy. I have question for you."

"Go ahead and ask. You can ask me anything."

"You like me?" Baby's face had the look of innocence as she spoke.

"Of course I like you. What do you mean?"

Baby looked at Cord intensely, "I mean, do you like me a lot?"

"Well yes, of course I do. Why you ask?"

"Because you not ask me out. I like go to dinner and movies, but you not ask. You just come to Chaise. I think you not like me."

Cord moved his arm from around her shoulder and stroked her hair. He looked her straight in the eyes and smiled. "You silly kid, I want to do all those things with you and more. I just didn't want to get you in trouble at the Chaise and maybe lose your job for seeing a customer." Cord sat back a little on the couch waiting for Baby's response.

"Why you not tell me? We can figure out. Oh that makes me happy. You really like me."

Cord moved his arm back around Baby and started to pull her closer when he winced, "Oh man! It's that shoulder of mine. If I keep it in one place too long and I get a twinge. It will pass in a minute." He began to rotate his arm back and forth.

"Let me see," Baby said as she put her tiny hands against his shoulder and began to rub. "That feel better?"

"It's starting to."

Baby stood up. She took Cord by the hand and led him to a bedroom with two twin beds, two small dressers and a mirror on the closet door.

"You give me shirt and lay down. I get lotion." Cord did as she asked. "This lotion is best. It makes pains go away. My feet and legs hurt after work. I rub them. It work for your shoulder."

Cord lay face down on the bed. Baby also got on the bed on her knees, one on each side of Cord's hips. She pressed out a small portion of lotion into the palm of her hand. She rubbed her hands together to warm it up. She gently massaged it in to Cord's shoulder.

Cord was amazed at the Baby's tender touch. It was soothing and sensual. Her soft hands were as smooth as the silk robe she wore. Cord exhaled a deep breath as she continued kneading the rest of his back. Her technique was putting him to sleep. She added pressure to the areas that felt stiff and knotted. She slowly transitioned her style of deep tissue to softly running her fingertips and nails over his back while brushing her long silk hair over his shoulders at the same time blowing softly across his back. She then leaned down close to him and whispered in his ear, "Turn over please."

Cord rolled over and noticed that Baby's robe was now unfastened exposing her bare brown body. He gazed upon her as if he was studying a work of art. "You are truly beautiful. You are a masterpiece that only the great masters could capture on canvas."

Baby pressed her body to Cord's while wrapping her arms around his shoulders. She kissed his neck and spoke softly into his ear, "I don't know what that mean. I love you Cord." With his arms around her waist Cord replied, "I love my little Morning Flower."

CHAPTER 13

P AGE SAT UP AT THE BAR bored and disinterested due to the lack of feeding opportunities at the Chaise. It was another slow Sunday. She had barely made cover and was hoping some of her regulars would show up. Most of the gentleman who were in that night were sitting close by the stage tossing dollars or watching sports at the bar while swigging the frothy foam of draft beer. Not even Mr. Freaky paid a visit and he was long overdue in her mind.

Page went up to the bar and ordered another shot of Patron for herself. She downed it with one swallow and then bit hard on a lemon slice. She looked up at the barmaid and said,

"I'll have another." A clean shot glass was put in front of her filled with tequila. Another lemon slice was added and a clean napkin next to her left hand. Page repeated the ritual and let out a cough before biting into the lemon.

"Sweets, I want to go home." There was a noticeable slight slur to her voice.

"Not yet, it's too early." The deep bass resounded.

"Come on, it's past ten and there is nothing happening. Besides I have already paid my cover."

"If it's still this slow at 11:30, you can go. Stay a little longer, you might get lucky." The corners of Sweet's mouth slowly expanded with a grin. Page had seen that grin numerous times before and knew there was no arguing with it.

As the evening progressed Page could hear the sound of opportunity. There was a pay-per-view boxing match on the television above the bar. Several patrons were betting amongst themselves. The noise at the bar was as loud as the cabaret music as one of the fighters on the screen hit the canvas and was down for the count.

"Yeah, I said he wouldn't last five rounds!" A patron hollered out, pumping his fist in the air. Page was siting a chair away from him when he got off the stool and grabbed her hand and said, "Come on, we are going to celebrate."

Page took him to a private booth and entertained him for four dances and pocketed $150 which included a $30 tip. She kissed him on the cheek and said, "Thanks baby, come again."

"You can count on it," he said as he made his way through the velvet curtains to the exit. Page could hear him whistling as he went out to the parking lot. The unexpected currency she now had uplifted her as if she downed three more shots of Patron. She was feeling pretty good. She looked over at Sweets with her arms out and palms up as if to say, "Well, how about it?"

Sweet smiled back and pointed to the girls' dressing room. It was a quarter to twelve and Page was happy to be getting out before 2:00 am. She made her way into the dressing room where a few of the girls were talking.

"Boy, you lucked out," one of the girls jealously spoke.

"Yeah." piped up another. "You were sitting in the right place at the right time. He would have taken anyone, even Phoenix!" The girls began to laugh.

"You bitches think you're funny," Phoenix replied. "I get plenty of guys. Otherwise why would I keep coming in?"

"Yeah, you get plenty of guys all right, but not many of them a second time unless they're old and forgetful." The laughter continued. Phoenix walked out of the dressing room towards the stage while raising her right arm up in the air with her back to them and flipping them off.

Page looked like a different person as she was escorted to her car. Gone was the makeup. The lingerie was carefully packed into her rollaway bag. Her blue jeans looked as though they had been spray painted on except for the torn threads at the knee and thigh. She looked like just any other young woman with a gray hoody and a light leather waistcoat. She left her white cross trainers untied.

She and Diamond rented a small two bedroom house close to downtown LA. It wasn't the most desirable area to live in, but the rent was reasonable and it was close to the Chaise. Also the parking was better than the other housing complexes nearby.

She parked her car and walked up to the front door. She didn't put a key in the lock; she turned the door knob back and forth a few times and she heard it unlock. "Obviously the landlord hadn't repaired the lock yet," she thought to herself. She had also asked that a bolt lock be put in as an extra measure of security but that hadn't happened either.

She went in the house and headed straight to her bedroom. She noticed the place was a mess. The dishes had not been done for a couple of days and clothes were strewn all over. She put her rollaway bag over near the closet door. Tossing her cap over towards her night stand she sat on the edge of her bed. She stepped on the back of her shoes in order to get them off and rubbed her feet. She removed her sweat shirt and reached inside her tank top to undo and take off her bra. She pulled her pants down which revealed the plaid male boxers she loved to wear. She walked over to her door and turned off the light. She made her way back to her bed and slumped face down on her pillow.

Page hadn't noticed the car trailing her a few lengths back as she drove home from the Chaise. Her radio was playing and she never heard the loud drone coming from the black sports car that parked a few doors away from her house. Trevor Johnson sat quietly in his late model Corvette as he bided his time waiting for the right moment.

After nearly 30 minutes, Trevor thought it was time. He carefully opened his car door and closed it without making a sound. He walked up to the front door. He remembered how Page played with the door knob. He turned it back and forth and pulled on it trying not to make any noise. The door opened. He let himself in while holding a knife in his right hand. He walked slowly towards the bedrooms but was unsure of where to go. He stopped for a moment.

"Diamond, is that you?" Page said groggily.

Trevor crept towards Page's bedroom. Page, rolling out of bed, thought she could make out a figure through the darkness and started towards the door to turn on the light. Trevor came through the door putting his left hand over her mouth and holding the knife to her throat.

"One word or scream bitch, and you are dead."

Page's eyes were filled with terror. She wanted to bite his hand or knee him in the groin, but Trevor's knife was pressed firmly under her chin. She dare not move.

"Ok, you," he said, "Let move over to the bed. I believe I've already paid for this."

"I won't fight you. Come on, let's get it over with," she muttered quietly.

Trevor pushed her over to the bed. As she fell he covered her throat in the grasp of his large left hand while still brandishing the knife before her eyes. He then slid his knife up one of the legs of her boxers and slit them. Page muffled out a cry out as she felt the cold blade on her thigh.

"I told you not a word bitch. Let's get to it. You know, do it like you mean it."

Page lay on the bead motionless as if void of any life. Trevor's eyes were full of fire as he angrily spoke, "I said do it like you mean it. You know, just like you pretend at the Chaise." He let go of her throat and punched her full force across her nose and cheek with his left hand. Page let out a shriek and began sobbing as tears comingled with the blood on her face. "Let's see how many dances that will get you." Trevor's rage was switched to a heightened level of excitement as he continued exerting his power and control.

"Please," she begged. "Don't hit me anymore. I'll do as you say." Page expelled reality from her mind as she began to perform. Her mind was empty, she blocked out all thoughts of the anguish she was experiencing. She prayed this would be a memory that could be erased as quickly as a bad dream or defecation flushed to the sewers.

Trevor began moaning in pleasure as he whispered to Page, "That's right, just like that. You're doing fine."

Diamond pulled up to the sidewalk of the apartment she and Page shared around 5:30 am. Her work at the Embassy was complete and she always returned around the light of day. She walked up the steps to the front door and noticed it was slightly open. "Damm," she thought to herself, "That slumlord needs to fix this useless lock." As she walked in she could hear soft sobs from the bedroom. As she drew closer to Page's bedroom she peered through the crack in the door. Page was lying on her side in a fetal position crying.

"Page, are you ok?"

"Don't touch me," she screamed.

Diamond flipped the light switch on the wall. "Oh my God!" she let out. "What happened?" Page was motionless and silent as Diamond surveyed the scene. Page's face was stained with blood. Her cheek was swollen and left eye nearly shut. Page turned to Diamond and moaned, "He raped me, that bastard raped me." Her tears flowed down her bloody cheeks as she cried.

Diamond sat down on the bed and embraced her sobbing friend. "Who, who did this to you?"

"The football jock. That asshole that comes to the club."

"That son of a bitch. OK, first things first, I'm taking you to a hospital to get you treated. I think your nose and jaw may be broken. I'll bring everything from the bed here. You can get a rape kit done and nail this piece of crap."

Page, sat up. "I'm not pressing charges, I can't.

"What, why the hell not?"

"It's no good Diamond. Think about where I work and how I entertain gentlemen."

"Gentlemen my ass. They are losers and scum," she blasted out.

"No I had a session with him at the club. He'll say I egged him on and I wanted it."

"He'll say you wanted your face beat in? I don't think so."

"He'll say I wanted it rough. It's no good, I'm not credible." Page shook he head. "Besides the police will probably dig up that I've turned a few tricks and don't forget, I have a record."

"That doesn't matter," snapped Diamond. "Well we are going to the hospital anyway. Come on, you need to be examined and put back together."

CHAPTER 14

MONDAY WAS GRUELING. DIAMOND WAITED WHILE the doctors and nurses attended to Page. Her nose was broken but her jaw was still intact. She would display a puffy purple cheek for a while as well as an enlarged dark circle around her left eye. Page remained silent as to the identity of her assailant although there was plenty of evidence, including the beating that Page had taken. The hospital had confirmed the sex as rape, not consensual, but Page refused to press charges.

Diamond stayed for several hours before heading back to the apartment. Everything that could be done for Page had been done. The police were gone, she had spoken with a counselor and she was now sedated. Diamond's hand shook as she turned the knob opening her front door. "What if he came back?" she thought. She knew the lock on the door wasn't reliable. "What if he is in there right now wanting to go another round?" Diamond's thoughts spun like a merry-go-round of terror imagining the worst possible scenarios.

She moved with caution while eyeing the unchanged disarray of clothes on the floor and dishes in the sink. She caught the faint scent of cigarettes that had been smoldering in the ashtray in the bedroom. The apartment was empty, she was safe. Her mind was calm until the shadow of guilt creeped in. "What if I had been here? Could I have stopped it? Maybe with two of us here he wouldn't have tried? Am I to blame?" She stopped questioning herself and poured herself a shot of gin and sat on her bed. She downed one, and then another. She went over to the front door and secured it with a kitchen chair under the doorknob. "No one is getting in this time," she thought. She walked over to her bed and fell on it hoping this nightmare would go away when she awoke.

Diamond rolled onto her side and checked the time. It was after eight, she had been asleep for several hours. Page was still at the hospital and nothing had changed. Page's bedroom framed unsightly images of the unspeakable. Her bed was stripped and the pillows were bare. Diamond couldn't get the sight of Page's attack out of her mind. She could see his filthy body on top of her. Diamond's throat grew cold as she could feel the knife against Page's throat. She became nauseous and ran into the bathroom, falling on her knees, clutching the side of the toilet. She vomited until her throat was dry. She couldn't stay in the house any longer. She washed her face and went out to her car. She drove to the one place where she could sort things out, the Chaise.

As she parted the velvet curtains, Diamond made her way to where Sweets was standing. "Can we talk?" She spoke softly as she pressed close to Sweets.

"Sure, I didn't expect to see you in today. What's up?"

"No, privately, back in your office."

Sweets and Diamond made their way past the bar, customers and stage to the office area. Sweets sat down behind a rosewood desk in a high-back, black leather chair. He leaned back with one foot on a desk drawer and asked, "Now what's going on?"

"It's Page, she's been raped." Diamond began to break down.

Sweets sat upright. "What the hell? When? Where?"

"At our house, early this morning, about 1:00 am."

"That's not long after her shift;, she left around midnight. Does she know who?"

Diamond wiped her eyes with her hands. "Oh she knows alright. It was that jock asshole; Trevor something." There was fire in her eyes as she spoke.

"I know the prick, I threw him out the other night for trying to stiff her. I punched up a bit on his credit card and told him not to come back." Sweets' brow was furrowed and his eyes looked cross. A mean scowl was developing across his face. "Is she pressing charges against the bastard?"

"No."

"Why, not? You've got evidence don't you?"

"Yeah, plenty. The problem is, Page feels based upon her lifestyle, past and present, she isn't credible, if you get my drift."

"Understood. How bad is she? Is she home yet?"

"She's pretty bad. Her face is all beat up and she was in shock when I found her around 5:30 this morning."

"Where the fuck were you?"

"I was out, ok! Besides, that is not the point. Something needs to be done."

Sweets, paused and let out a breath. "You mean you want me to do something…?"

"Come on man, I know you have connections." Diamond put her hand on top of Sweets' shoulder. He patted it with his other hand and smiled. "Shit… well I don't know about that." His deep voice resonated. "This sounds like a police matter to me, but I'll check with my so called connections as you say. If I hear anything, I'll let you know." Sweets grinned a half smile. "Tell Page to get as much rest and help as she needs. Her job will always be here."

"Thanks babe, you're the best. I'll see you Wednesday night. I'm going back to the hospital."

CHAPTER 15

————————●

I T WAS AFTER TEN WHEN DIAMOND arrived at the hospital. Visiting hours were over but Diamond managed to gain the security guard's sympathy and allowed her to go into see Page. The bed beside her was empty. Previously, a victim from an accidental shooting was her roommate, but the patient had been released. Page had her bed at a 45 degree angle and looked fast asleep while lying flat on her back. She had an IV in her right arm. Her facial features had improved somewhat with the cleaning up. Her face was a colored kaleidoscope of purple, blue and black tones under her left eye which still had signs of swelling. The medications had eliminated some of the puffiness in her cheek.

Diamond moved the blue guest chair closer to the side of Page's bed and moved her uneaten food tray aside. Page rolled towards Diamond and slowly opened her lethargic eyes. Diamond reached out with her right hand and softly rubbed the top of Page's left. "How you holding up girl?" There was kindness in her voice. "When are you getting out of here?"

With a slurred speech Page slowly spoke, "I'm going home tomorrow. Everyone was here forever. They kept asking me the same questions over and over while telling me what I should do. I lost it and started screaming. That's when they gave me the needle. They probably thought I was going to kill someone or myself. I'm ok now."

"Do you want me to come get you?"

"No, my sister and her husband are coming down from Riverside. I'm going back to their place. I'm done Diamond. Done with the Chaise, done with our house and done with LA."

"Well what are you going do girl?"

"I don't know. I'll think of something, just not now. I'm really tired. Call me on my cell tomorrow night." Page turned away from Diamond and laid flat on her back once again closing her eyes.

Diamond left the hospital and walked out to her car. It never occurred to her that Page would be moving out although it made sense. Her mind was a whirlwind of confusion and unanswered questions. She sat in her car trying to make sense of everything that had transpired in the last two days.

She wondered if she was vulnerable and at risk being at the house all alone. Would Trevor come back and try to put another notch on his gun? Would she need to find another roommate now that her rent had just doubled? Who could she stand to live with? Page was the perfect roommate. She kept to herself and was easy to get along with and always paid her share.

She started up the car and began the drive home. She was still nervous as she pulled up alongside of the house. She walked slowly up the three steps to the front door. She cautiously worked the door knob to verify the door was still locked and hadn't been tripped. She unlocked the door and opened it to a slight crease while standing on the step and reached inside to the light switch on the wall. She peered into the front room trying to ease her paranoia. The room was empty; she walked in and locked the front door behind her.

She explored the rest of the interior. She started with the kitchen, moved to the bathroom and then checked out the bedrooms until she had satisfied herself all was clear. She went back to the kitchen, pulled a glass out of the cupboard, filled it with ice and poured what was left in the bottle of gin sitting on the counter. It wasn't much, but it was what she needed. After downing a couple of swallows she breathed a sigh with the knowledge she was alone and safe.

As Diamond became more rational in her thoughts she realized that she could no longer stay at this house. She knew she could never be comfortable or at peace here. She would always think about Page and Trevor and if he was going to come back. She hated to leave not only because it was inconvenient due to the timing, (she wanted to keep focus on playing Johnny) but moving was a pain in the ass was. The rent was low and it was only about 15 minutes from the Chaise. The neighborhood was ok and she and Page had never had any problems until now.

The thought of having to move really bothered Diamond. She dreaded filling out apps, credit checks, packing all her stuff, then loading and unloading and putting everything away. She also knew it would most likely cost more if she found a nicer place in a better neighborhood.

Diamond knew there was going to be a money issue. She would have to come up with a deposit and at some places the landlords wanted first and last month rent as well. She had a bit in savings but did not want to tap into that. She thought she might have to pick up more nights at the Chaise or turn a few more tricks. Then the lightbulb of revelation lit up – Johnny. She was sure she could get Johnny to help her out. Once again she would turn to Johnny, her knight in shining armor, her conquering hero, and the answer to her problems.

CHAPTER 16

WORK WAS TAKING ITS TOLL ON Johnny. Hours of testing and quality assurance results were inconsistent. The X-Lab project was still behind schedule. The configuration problems in the product data had not been resolved. Johnny had 2 months to deliver a working prototype which he considered impossible. He saw his head nailed to a post for all to see along with the other failed managers. He was the lead in Puccini's Turandot and had no answer for the riddles.

He thought of his highly successful career ending on a disastrous note that not only stained his reputation but had serious financial impact to the company. His desk was littered with code printouts, schematics, flow charts and project plans. The errors during the prototype's testing could not be duplicated with each test. They were hit and miss. Some were successful and others were not. There was no common thread they could point to. Johnny left his briefcase and the printouts on his desk. He walked out of RayCom and headed to his car.

Johnny started up the car and turned on the CD player. He had Debussy in and hoped that would calm him and alleviate some of his stress. It was after 7:00 when he pulled up the driveway to his house. The rush hour traffic had already passed so it didn't take him as long to get home. Upon opening the front door he took a few steps and let out with a groan. He had stepped on a small metal truck.

"Are the boys still here?" he questioned in a loud voice.

"No, they left about 2 hours ago why?"

Johnny looked about the entry hall and the front room, there were toys scattered everywhere. Balls, skates, books, and super-hero figures, the carpet was laden with them.

"Damm it, why didn't they pick up their toys? This place looks like a dump." There was a hint of anger in Johnny's voice.

"Maddy was late and just whooshed them away. I told her I would clean up."

"I see." Johnny continued surveying what to him was a battlefield of carnage. He just shook his head and walked into the kitchen and kissed Jenny on her forehead. "I'm sorry," he said.

"I've got your dinner ready for you. Meatloaf, just the way you like it with bar-b-que sauce on top and a baked potato. Would you like some carrots or broccoli?"

"No, just some of the meatloaf and the potatoes will be fine. Do we have any beer, I could use a beer."

"Don't be silly dear, we hardly ever have beer. You have never been much of a beer drinker."

"Well I'm likely to be now." Johnny's tone was less angry although it was obvious something was bothering him.

"What is wrong honey, is it work?"

"Oh it is work alright. If I explained it to you with all the details, it would only confuse you and you would ask a dozen questions. I will give it to you in the simplest terms possible: my project is failing. I am going to miss delivery and I might lose my job. There you have it. Do not ask me any questions."

"I'm so sorry dear, I know I'm no help in these matters." Jenny placed Johnny's dinner in front of him along with a glass of milk.

"I work hard all day, I am under so much pressure and stress I am about to explode like Vesuvius. Is it too much to ask that I come home to a clean house after a hard day's work?"

Jenny had no response. She did not know how to react. This was a side of Johnny she had never seen. In all their years of marriage he never raised his voice to her, criticized her or put her down. She didn't know whether to cry or leave the room. She walked back towards the stove and with her back to Johnny and a lump in her throat replied, "I'm sorry. I guess I just forgot about the mess while I was preparing dinner." Johnny looked up her and could see she was hurt. "Forgive me, I do not know what came over me. I'm just not myself these days."

Johnny began to eat. "The meatloaf is good, thanks." When he was done eating he took his plate over to the sink and rinsed it off. He then rinsed out his glass and placed it next to his plate on the sink. "I need a shower," he called out as he left the kitchen and walked up the stairs to the master bedroom and into the shower.

When Johnny got into the bathroom, he looked in the mirror and noticed he needed a shave. His hair was a disheveled array of untidy fibers. As he reflected on his unsightly appearance, reality awakened him. With all the stress and problems of work and home, he had completely forgotten what day it was. It was Wednesday.

He had lost track of the days due to the tedious and sometimes chaotic routine at work and the boredom he found at home. Now he was ready to embark on his other life, his fantasy. The fantasy he so wished was reality. A fantasy that could pull him out of the drudgery known as his life. The Chaise was calling him, he would answer that call and Diamond would be waiting. She would take him to that other world from which he never wanted to return, the world of pleasure.

After Johnny showered, he put on his charcoal wool slacks and a polo shirt. He left the top button open. He slipped on his loafers without socks, combed his hair and brushed his teeth. His designer cologne brought him back to life as he dabbed it on. He walked down the stairs to the front door and called out, "I'm going out, I need some air." Jenny did not answer.

The parking lot at the Chaise was moderately full. It was what one would expect on a Wednesday night at 10:00 pm. Johnny paid his cover and made his way in. His eyes needed a moment or two to adjust to the dark. The undiscernible lyrics along with the reverberating bass that bounced off every wall did not seem to bother Johnny anymore. He found a booth, far from the stage and the bar. He prized his solitude and enjoyed hiding in the shadows until Diamond would make an appearance.

Diamond was sitting in the ladies dressing room with her feet up on a chair and a bottled water in her hand. Phoenix entered the room with a smug smirk, walked over to Diamond and said, "Hey, your man is here, you going to take him again?"

"Of course, but not yet. I'm not ready for him. I'll make him wait for me while I work on my strategy for a couple more minutes. The longer he waits, the more he will want me and the more he'll spend."

"What if another gal grabs his attention, what then?" a voice from the back laughed.

"No one else could, he only has eyes for me. I think he is falling for me. It is all part of the game, and I'm winning." Diamond got up and sat down at the vanity section and checked her makeup. She applied a dash more rouge and painted her lips. She sprayed a spot of perfume to her neck, then played with her hair. She admired herself closely in the mirror and said to herself, "Oh yeah, I'm winning." She winked at her reflection and bowed to the other ladies in the dressing room as if expecting applause.

Sweets was walking around the club making sure everything was on the up and up. He would occasionally turn a blind eye if he thought a worker and a client were enjoying themselves possibly beyond the limits of legality behind the curtains. As far as he was concerned, they were consenting adults and if the girl was ok with the activity, he would just keep walking. He stopped when he approached two of his bouncers, Ray and Ellis, who were standing near the stage.

"Guys, come here."

"What's up?"

"Yeah, what's up?"

"Listen guys, we had a problem a few nights back. Some asshole hurt one of my girls."

"What did he do to her?"

"Who did it, what girl?"

"Never mind the girl or what happened. That is none of your damm business." Sweets regained his composure. "You remember that football prick I threw out last week?"

"I remember him," said Ray, "Yeah, a real arrogant ass."

"Yeah but he's got one hell of an arm," remarked Ellis.

"OK, you know who I'm talking about."

"What do you want us to do?"

Sweets looked at them both, "I don't know that I want you to do anything. I will bet since he is not allowed in here anymore he's down at 4-Play. Just thought you two ought to know."

"Thanks Sweets. You wouldn't mind if we went out for a snack in about an hour would you?" Ray winked.

"No, be my guest.

Diamond came out of the ladies room and found Johnny. In her mind, he couldn't have picked a more perfect place for her to wield her charms and poison. As she approached Johnny, he started to stand up. Diamond put a hand to his shoulder and said, "Oh sit down hun, we are way past that." She sat as close as possible to Johnny and while hugging his arm, she kissed him on the cheek.

"I was hoping you would come," There was sadness in her voice as she rubbed noses with him. "It has been a slow night and I really needed to see you, you know, someone I care about and trust."

"Well, I'm here and I really needed to see you too. I've missed you. What can I do for you?"

"I don't think there's anything you or anyone can do for me. I still have trouble talking about it. I'm so scared."

"Scared of what? What happened? Tell me."

Diamond buried her face on Johnny's shoulder and whispered in his ear, "It's Page, she's been raped." Diamond raised her head and looked Johnny in the eyes, "You can't tell anybody. Promise me you won't tell anybody"

"You are kidding! How did it happen?"

"No I'm not! Promise me."

"I promise. How did it happen?"

"It was late Sunday night and Page was still at work. I couldn't sleep for some reason and got up and went out for a drive. I was gone for maybe an hour, maybe two. When I came back, I noticed the front door was cracked open and I found Page on the bed, bloodied and in shock. I got her to the hospital, she was in bad shape."

"Who did this? How did they get in?"

"Page doesn't know who did it. He had his face covered. All she remembers is he had a knife and held it at her throat. I'll tell you how he got in. Our door lock is flakey, and the landlord hasn't fixed it. Sometimes if you play with the knob just right, the door unlocks."

"This is terrible. I am shocked. Is she going to be alright?"

"I guess, she is off with her sister in Riverside now. Johnny, I am so scared, I just can't go back there now. What if he comes back? What if he comes and I'm all alone? I've got to get out of there and find another place."

"You are right, I don't think you should go back there. There are some other nice apartments down Santa Monica Boulevard."

"Oh, Johnny, I don't have enough money for those. You're talking $2,000.00 a month. Our house was $1,600.00 and Page was paying half of that."

"Well I have got a friend who has some apartments that are nice, and in a good neighborhood. He might be willing to give me a deal. Can you stay at a hotel for a few nights while I see if I can get you setup with something?"

"That would be great, but I'm strapped for cash right now. I'm probably going to have to work a couple more nights to make ends meet."

Johnny reached in his pocket and pulled out several twenty dollar bills folded over. "Here's $200. That should hold you over for a few days. I'll come back Friday night and let you know what I have found out about an apartment."

"Oh you are such a dear, yes that will hold me. How about you holding me now for a while?" Diamond pressed herself against Johnny and put one hand up to his cheek. "I love you Johnny."

It was nearly 11:00 when Ray and Ellis pulled up to the 4-Play. It is a smaller club with fewer amenities than the Chaise. It is a dive. No flashing neon, or bright lights, just a dimly lit sign above the front door in a cursive script that read: *4-Play.*

There were only about 30 cars in the parking lot. 4-Play did not enjoy the kind of popularity and clientele as the Chaise. It was located in a seedier part of town not far from East LA. Ray and Ellis drove at a slow speed around the parking lot eyeing all the cars.

"There," pointed Ray, "What do you think?" Ellis stopped the car for a moment while inspecting a black, late model Corvette. The license plate read: "GOLONG"

"I think that's our man Ray." Ellis grinned and Ray winked back at him.

"OK Ray, we'll park up the street and walk down to the club. First you go in then me. Once we get in, we'll figure what our next move is."

"Works for me."

Ellis parked the car about a block away from the club. Ray entered the club first followed by Ellis a couple of minutes later. Unlike the Chaise, 4-play had no cover charge which was obvious after entering. The interior was run-down and forgotten. The decor had not been updated in several years and smacked of a condemned theater. There were round tables with chairs similar to the Chaise but not as nice or as comfortable. The only redeeming features were the velvet nude paintings on the walls that brought back memories of the 80s weekend flea markets.

There were about eight girls working the floor and there may have been others in the dressing room. Three of the girls were sitting at the bar chatting amongst themselves rather than mingling with gentlemen who appeared as if they had little to offer. There were a number of men scattered throughout the club. Most were sitting by themselves, spaced a good distance from each other. There were a few men who had girls sitting with them enjoying the entertainment.

The girls at 4-Play were not what you would call sleazy, but they were not in the same esthetic class as the girls from the Chaise. Nonetheless, they were still attractive enough to bring in customers.

Ray and Ellis did not sit near each other. They chose to remain as anonymous as possible in the club. No girls came and sat by them, their body language appeared closed to the dancers. Ray spied Trevor a few rows back from the stage. From time to time he would get up and throw dollar bills at whomever was dancing. One girl, a blond with a pale face and large breasts sat down next to Trevor and began stroking his forearm with her fingertips while whispering in his ear. Within minutes, they both stood up and made their way over to a private room.

Ray stood up, unnoticed by anyone, and wandered over to Trevor's chair. There was a black leather blazer draped over its back. Ray sat down and moved his hands into the front side pockets of Trevor's coat. He felt keys in his right hand. "I love it when it's easy," he thought to himself. He took out his cell phone and texted Ellis, "Send me a text when he is leaving." With that he walked out of the club and headed towards the black corvette.

Trevor was in the private room for fifteen minutes. He came out, hugged his girl and went over to his table. He picked up his drink and downed it. He put on his jacket and started to walk out of the club. Ellis immediately texted Ray, "Here he comes."

Trevor walked out of the club mildly intoxicated but still able to walk straight and not have the appearance he had put down several drinks earlier. He noticed his car was not where he had parked it. He wondered was he really so drunk he could not remember where he parked? The parking lot was not that large and he could not believe his car was not there. He reached in his pocket for the keys to sound his alarm and came up empty. "Where are my keys? What the... oh crap my car has been stolen!" he thought. As he reached for his cell he heard the loud roar of his engine and saw his car speeding directly towards him. He tried to move out of the way as the car accelerated, but to no avail. He felt the car clip his right knee which sent him hurtling through the air in the parking lot until he hit the ground while the car sped off.

Folks immediately came pouring out of the club to see Trevor vomiting on the ground with his right leg bent while he clutched his knee. Ray drove the corvette down an alley unseen. He parked the car and left the keys on the floor. He walked back to where he and Ellis had parked their car earlier and found Ellis in the driver's seat waiting for him. Ray immediately slid in his seat and buckled up while Ellis drove them back to the Chaise.

CHAPTER 17

T HURSDAY WAS ANOTHER DAY FILLED WITH the same played out meetings that brought up the same trivial issues that never went anywhere except to schedule more meetings. Johnny walked the floor observing the partitioned cages which housed the employees at work. The cubicles reminded him of 60's folksinger and songwriter Malvina Reynolds. As far as Johnny was concerned, Malvina was a visionary when she wrote "Little Boxes". Johnny heard the sound of employees entering in test data and coding away at their keyboards. Johnny made his way up to Ron Crocker's office and knocked on the open door.

"Got lunch plans?"

"No, where were you thinking?"

"I've got a hankering for a meatball sandwich."

"Sounds like a trip to Ernie's. I'm in."

Ernie's was a local Italian restaurant known for its foot long sandwiches and zesty Italian meats and sauces. It had been a staple for years and was usually packed for lunch. Johnny and Ron left RayCom around 11:00 to ensure they would get a seat. The sun was vibrant and the temperature had taken a drop and was now in the low seventies. A cloudless, light blue sky with the San Gabriel Mountains in view made the perfect backdrop for a pleasant lunch.

Johnny ordered his meatball sandwich with marinara and provolone and Ron had the six meat cold cuts with two cheeses. They both ordered chips and bottled water to go along with their subs. They took their lunches to the outdoor patio and basked in the warm LA sunshine.

"You know what would make this perfect Johnny? A couple of beers," Ron sighed.

"There's no reason why we can't. The rule is you can have a beer at lunch, just don't go back to work."

"Sounds like win, win to me! So what's on your mind boss? I know you enjoy my company but your face tells me you want something."

"Yeah, you read me like a book. I'm worried Ron. This X-Lab project is getting to me. I can't understand what we are doing wrong."

"We are not doing anything wrong. We've turned this thing inside and out. I don't believe it's on our end. I believe the vendor software we are using is corrupting the product data manager when we try to configure the effectivity."

"Which vendor?"

"ProSoft"

"Our PDM?" Good grief. And we are in contract negotiations as we speak. I have been arguing that their bid is too high and unreasonable and they have not dealt with the issues we have reported.

"What is their response?"

"Supposedly, everything has been corrected in the next release. It is in beta now and won't be in production for another three months."

"See if you can get them to allow us to test the beta, maybe we will find something." Ron picked up his bottled water and downed a few swallows.

"I tried, but they said no. They don't believe our problem is their problem. They know we cannot switch vendors and move all the product data. Besides, they know they have a uniqueness that we take advantage of which is part of our competitive edge. They know we cannot give that up. We are deep in the sheets with them unfortunately." Johnny took another bite of his sandwich.

"Yeah, you are right. Well here's my thought, I'm going to put Dana Pulley on the ProSoft configuration and integration with our PDM. She is the expert in that area."

"I know she is, but she is a lone wolf who does things her way and has no respect for protocol or procedures. But you are right and I am desperate. Get her on it."

"Will do as soon as we get back to the office, provided we do not order any beer!"

"You're funny. Something else I wanted to ask you about."

"Ok, go ahead."

"You still have a number of properties you are managing?"

"Yes, I still have a few apartments I rent out, why?"

"I have a friend who is down on his luck right now. He lost his job a few weeks ago and he needs a place. I hate to ask you for a favor, but have you got any available right now?"

Ron held up his hand to pause Johnny while finished another bite. He moved forward in his chair, closer to the table as whispered to Johnny, "Got something on the side, have you?"

"No, no, this is on the level. I am just trying to help the guy out."

"You are in luck, I have had this small two bedroom, one bath available for about three months and no takers. Nice little place in a good neighborhood. It is right around Washington."

"How, much are you asking?

"Two grand."

Johnny shook his head. "I couldn't afford that."

"What, you are going to pay?"

"Only until he gets on his feet. Just a few months, and then he can take over."

"Johnny, you never cease to amaze me, you are too good. I tell you what. I will charge you $500 a month for the first four months then charge your friend a grand once he is flush. No, deposit or anything else, how does that sound?"

"You would do that for me, Ron?" Johnny said in a stutter.

"Sure, what are best friends for anyway? You would do the same for me, right? Besides it is empty, any money I get is gravy."

Johnny nodded and held out his hand for Ron's. As they shook hands, Johnny said, "I cannot thank you enough, I don't even know how to thank you."

"No worries," smiled Ron. "We better get back to work before we order those beers!"

They walked out of Ernie's with toothpicks in their teeth, heading back to the car. All Johnny could think of was, "Wait until I tell Diamond."

Friday night couldn't come soon enough for Johnny. He was bursting with excitement to give Diamond the good news. He would really be her hero now. More than that, he saw himself as her savior. After all, she said she loved him, and Johnny took that to heart and believed her. He was convinced he was in love with her as well.

He imagined what Diamond's reaction would be when he would tell her about the apartment. She would throw her arms around him and cover him with kisses. She might even cry for joy. What if she suggested he move in with her, he thought. Could he do it? Could he give up the life he had known for the past 35 years? How could he manage it? He thought he had enough in savings and his 401K that he could give Jenny whatever she needed and he could get by. But what about the emotional impact? What would this do to Jenny? This would be an unsuspecting bombing. She had no idea and this would shatter her. Johnny felt she did not deserve this and even though he felt he was no longer in love with her, he still loved her and did not want to hurt her. He dismissed these thoughts as he pulled into the Chaise parking lot.

There was a good crowd at the Chaise that night due to another pay-per-view sporting event that was being televised at the bar. He noticed Diamond at the bar sitting by herself in her best lingerie wearing a blue silk robe that barely graced her exposed thighs.

"Hey, how are you," Johnny smiled. There was a confident look about him that Diamond had not seen before. This sent up a red flag. Diamond thought she was the one in control, calling the shots and leading Johnny to whatever snare she laid out. This made her uncomfortable.

"Hi hun, I'm doing fine. Good to see you." She took her time as she gathered her thoughts.

"Come on, let's get a booth, I've got some news for you. Let me buy some drinks. Bombay Sapphire and scotch on the rocks," Johnny called out as he signaled a waitress.

Diamond was apprehensive as she heard Johnny call out a drink for her. "What gives?" she thought. "What has come over him?" Her defenses went up.

"Sure, love, that sounds great."

Johnny took Diamond by the arm and walked her over to a booth away from the crowd. A waitress brought over the drinks and Johnny gave her thirty dollars and said, "Keep it."

Diamond took a sip from her glass and said, "Ok, what is all the excitement about?" as she tried to regain control again.

Johnny pulled out a key and put it on the table. "Do you know what this is?"

"No. The key to the executive washroom?" She laughed.

"No my dear, it is the key to your new apartment."

Diamond was dumbstruck. She didn't know what to say. She just looked at Johnny with eyes glazed, wondering how to respond. She took a deep swallow of her drink. "What do you mean Johnny?"

"It is yours. I told you I had a friend who had some property. It is all taken care of and paid for." Johnny took a card out of his pocket, "Here's the address."

"Oh Johnny, you shouldn't have." This was not part of Diamond's plan. Johnny was supposed to keep feeding her money and she would find her own place. She did not want one that he arranged and certainly not one where he knew the address.

Johnny spoke up, "I knew the surprise would be too much for you. If you need help packing or moving out, just let me know. It is a pretty nice place, I checked it out, two bedrooms, one bath, in a good section of town. I think you'll like it. More important, you will be safe there.

"Johnny, you are so good to me and I really don't deserve it. Let's get a private room for thirty minutes and let me show you my appreciation."

"That sounds good, I would really like to be alone with you, even if it is only for a little while."

"It will cost $300. I hate to ask, but it is my job you know."

Johnny, took the cash from his sterling silver money clip and handed it to Diamond. He felt like a big shot and a total hero. He did not get the reaction he hoped for from Diamond but things would be different in the private room. There he would tell her he loved her.

Diamond walked over near the bar where Sweets was standing. She handed him the money, "Private for thirty minutes." Sweets nodded.

"Oh by the way," Diamond spoke up, "I read in the paper that jock got hit by a car, his own car in fact." Sweets raised his brow ever so slightly and said, "Yeah, I read that too."

CHAPTER 18

THE DAYS CONTINUED AT RAYCOM WITH little progress on the X-Lab project. Cord had decided around 11:00 to take an early and extended lunch. He drove downtown towards Baby's apartment. It wouldn't take long and traffic was light at that hour. It was hard for him to concentrate on his driving. His mind flashed through scenes of him and Baby together. His heart raced to the car's acceleration the closer he got to Baby's.

Their affair was now approaching two months. Each encounter increased with passion and ecstasy. Baby continued to ask Cord why they would only meet at her place or the club. She wondered why they didn't go on dates, the movies or dinners together like other couples. Cord assured her that time would come but he was under a lot of pressure at work and was working all kinds of ridiculous hours. Cord was convincing in his lies.

Cord parked outside of the apartment and grabbed the bottle of chardonnay he had brought with him. He knew Baby liked having wine when they were together and it seem to work like an aphrodisiac after a couple of glasses.

Baby opened the door slightly standing behind it allowing Cord to enter. Cord's eyes were all over her. Baby had on a silk white sleep shirt buttoned at the waist and a pair of white laced bikini briefs. She was barely covered. Her long raven black hair adorned her shoulders. She was barefoot. With his thumb and index finger, Cord lifted up her chin to him and gently kissed her. "I'll get us a couple glasses," and he went into the kitchen.

"I don't want wine, Cord. I'll just have water."

"Really, I thought you really enjoyed it. Are you ok? You're not sick are you?"

"Oh no, I think water better for me now. Cord, I have something to tell you. Promise you not get angry?"

Cord set the chardonnay on the counter. He had a puzzled look on his face. He was sure Baby was calling it quits and their time was over.

"My little morning flower, you can tell me anything. What's wrong?"

"I pregnant," she blurted out.

There was a solemn darkness to Cord's face as she spoke those words. It was if he had just been shot point blank in the gut. His body was tightening, he felt his fists clenching. His jaw was locked, he was at a loss for words He could not even conjure up a lie. He peered into Baby's dark eyes and replied, "I don't know what to say. I never thought …"

"It ok." Baby stroked his cheek with her soft palm and calmly continued. "You love me, yes?"

"Of course I do, but I, this, well I just wasn't…"

Baby stopped him as he spoke. "We can get married, I love you Cord. I quit the Chaise and find another job."

Cord's expression was stern now. He grabbed ahold of Baby's arms with his two hands.

"We cannot get married."

"Why? We love each other, what the problem."

"The problem my love is I am already married."

Tears were forming in Baby's eyes and she spoke. "Married," she bawled, "Why you not tell me? Why you do this to me?" She broke loose of Cord holding her arms.

"I did not mean for this to happen. I thought we were just two people enjoying each other. I never expected this. I figured sooner or later we would just go our own way."

Baby wiped her face with both hands. "What we do now? I not want baby without husband."

As Cord faced the reality of his dilemma he opened up, "I can help you. I will pay to help for you to get rid of it if you want."

"Now you make me murderer? Get out, take this with you." She shoved the bottle of wine in Cord's chest. "You not come back. I no want see you." She walked over to the door and opened it, and looked at Cord with her red drenched eyes, "Get out."

Baby went to the Chaise on Friday night as if nothing had changed in her life. She hoped that the attention of clients, both new and old would get her mind off things. She wanted to find Diamond and ask her for advice. She was sure Diamond would know how to deal with the situation.

Diamond arrived around 10:00. Baby found her in the dressing room preparing for the night. "Diamond, we need talk, private." Diamond sensed there was something wrong." Give me a couple of minutes kid and then we can go out the back pretending to have a smoke." Diamond finished getting herself ready and she went out the back door of the dressing room with Baby to a secluded, gated section of the parking lot.

"OK, what's troubling you?"

"I pregnant."

Diamond felt like telling her, "I warned you," but kept that to herself. "I'm sorry, you poor thing. Who is the father?"

"It Cord, and he married."

"Son of a bitch! These pigs are all alike. What did he suggest?"

"He say I should get rid of it. He offer to pay, but I no want to kill baby. I not know what to do."

"How far along are you? Do you know?" Diamond was pulling Baby into her confidence.

"I think six weeks, why?

Diamond had a solution. Baby was not the first unwed mother she knew of who needed help. There were a couple of other girls working at the Chaise in the last year that had a similar situation.

Diamond put her hands on Baby's shoulders until their eyes were locked upon each other. "I know a doctor who can prescribe a medication. It is two pills. It is not an operation and it is natural. You will have a miscarriage."

"So I no murder my baby?"

"No, you will not. At six weeks, it is not a baby. You will have some cramping, and a little bleeding, just like your period and then it is over."

Baby had never heard of this. She was not sure if the pills were right, but she trusted Diamond. "Ok, I think I do that."

"Alright kid, leave everything to me."

The wheels began to turn as Diamond's conning mind was concocting another plan.

On Saturday, Johnny sat at the kitchen table with his coffee. He was solemn. He thought about how he and Jenny were growing apart. Very seldom did they eat together and when they did, they sat at opposite ends of the table instead of directly across from each other. Their conversation was limited and could be described as small talk at best. They did not argue. They appeared to be a couple that had just run out of things to say to each other.

"Would you like some breakfast?" Jenny asked.

"No thanks, I am not really hungry right now. I will fix a sandwich or something else later." Jenny began to spread some cream cheese on her bagel. Johnny poured himself another cup of coffee.

"You got any plans today?" He asked.

"I thought Maddy and I would take the boys to the park. It is going to be another nice day. How about you?"

"Oh, I will probably take a walk or a drive. Maybe catch up on some of my reading. I am going to have to lock myself up in the office for a bit. I have got a lot of work to do on this project you know. It is not looking good. Anyway, it should all be over in a couple of months. I have filled out my retirement papers. I haven't put them in, but they are ready. Depending on how this project ends up I might be asked to submit them."

"Is it that bad? They would ask you to resign?"

"You bet, someone has to take the blame if this project fails. Right now all fingers seem to be pointing my way."

"Can we make it?" Jenny had a worried tone in her voice. There was a look of uncertainty in her eyes.

"Sure, we will be fine. The house is paid for and we have got plenty in savings. There is also my 401K and my company pension. We will be alright. Don't worry about it. I think I will go for a drive now." Johnny grabbed his keys and without saying good-bye, he was gone.

Johnny was off to Seventh Street and headed for the 10 West, the Santa Monica Freeway. Traffic was light and within minutes he exited on to the Pacific Coast Highway heading towards Malibu. He loved the thirty-five mile drive with the hills to the right of him and the ocean to the left. He drove the curves and bends on the single lane highway for approximately forty minutes until he arrived at his destination: Paradise Cove.

He couldn't remember the last time he was there. Johnny loved this place. He would sit under an umbrella at a redwood picnic table on the sand. Johnny picked out his spot with a scenic view of the waves crashing against the rocks and rolling across the sand. He kicked off his topsiders and dug his feet into the warm sand.

The waiter come out with his cordial, friendly greetings, said his name was Brian and placed a pitcher and a large wine glass of ice water graced with a lemon wedge on the side on the table. He then handed Johnny a menu. "I will give you a couple of minutes to browse and decide."

Johnny thanked the waiter as he returned to the restaurant. Johnny looked at the menu but he knew what he wanted. It had been a couple of years, but he had not forgotten the magnificent entre that enticed his palate the last time he was here: clam chowder with Dungeness crab and grilled cheese. He began to salivate just thinking of it.

Johnny had two glasses of chardonnay to go with his meal. It was early to be drinking but the chardonnay with chowder was like Gershwin with a piano: paradise found. He wiped the bowl clean with the last quarter of his grilled cheese. He was satisfied he had done something for himself for a change. He loved watching the waves come and go. He was at one with the tide and could sit there mesmerized for hours, deep in his thoughts. Jenny did not share his love of the beach. She was of the opinion it was always too windy and the sand was bothersome and hard to walk on. The ocean was always too cold for her taste. She just didn't understand the attraction.

That was fine with Johnny, he treasured the solitude while inhaling the salty air and studying the immensity of the sea.

Johnny had been out almost three hours by the time he got home. Jenny was gone. She and Maddy were at some nearby park letting the boys burn as much energy as possible. Sunset was painting the horizon when Jenny returned home. "Oh those boys." She said as she shook her hair. "I did not think they would ever wear down," She closed the front door.

"Well they are boys! What did you expect?" Johnny laughed, he thought it felt good to laugh again.

"Do you need me to fix you any dinner?" Jenny asked politely.

"No, I am still stuffed from that incredible lunch." Johnny patted his stomach.

"Where did you go?"

"To paradise." Johnny smiled.

"What?"

"Paradise Cove, up in Malibu."

"Oh, the beach, good for you. Well I am not hungry either, in fact I am worn out. I will just have a salad and some fruit."

"I think I will go into my office and work on the computer for a while. Then I'll probably go for another drive to unwind."

"Whatever." Jenny remarked.

"Yeah, whatever." Johnny sighed as he walked back to his office.

Johnny brought up several pieces of his financial data that he had tracked in spreadsheets. He made sure everything was up to date. His savings was down a bit due to his spending on Diamond at the Chaise, but he felt he was still in good shape. He had invested wisely over the years and had recently moved all his assets to low ventures. He had most of his bills on auto pay. He monitored his savings and would transfer funds to his checking account as needed.

Johnny began to ponder the possibility of leaving Jenny. He would guarantee that she would be taken care of financially. He needed to write up how he took care of the finances. Jenny needed to understand the monthly bills and how they were paid. She also needed to know other ways to access their money besides the ATM.

Johnny spent a good two hours working up instructions and details for Jenny including who to contact on his life insurance for when the time came. Johnny needed to take time to instruct Jenny on the computer and bring her up to speed on the family finances if he thought he ever were to leave her. Jenny was not knowledgeable about technology and thought the computer hated her.

Johnny straightened up his office. He thought about getting himself ready to go to the Chaise. As he was putting his papers and files back in their place in his desk drawers, he pulled out one drawer and saw something he had long forgotten about, his 38 revolver.

Johnny wasn't much of a gun advocate and got the gun from a friend years ago during the Rodney King riots. Johnny put it away as soon as it was given to him and later registered it. Everything was legal. He didn't like it in the house, especially with the two boys. They never went in his office, but there was always a chance they could go in there and they were curious. He wanted to avoid tragedy at all costs.

Johnny decided he wanted it out of the house. Then a great idea came to him. He would give it to Diamond. After all, she was alone and probably would feel safer with it for protection. Johnny's mind was made up, he would take it with him tonight and surprise her.

Johnny arrived at the Chaise around 9:30, it was pretty packed. He made his way in and found a booth near the dressing room. He sat down and waited for Diamond to arrive.

Johnny hadn't been sitting long when a dark African-American girl came up to him.

"Mind if I sit down?"

Johnny looked up surprised to see someone other than Diamond vying for his attention. The girl was young and pretty. She shined like polished patents. Her black hair hung to her shoulders. It was coarse, but not nappy. Before Johnny could answer she held out her hand and said, "I'm Hershey."

"Johnny," he replied as he stood up and shook her hand.

Hershey sat down next to Johnny and scooted close to him. "I'm new here, have you been in before?" She ran her fingertips over Johnny's hair.

"I guess you could say I am somewhat of a regular. I come in from time to time to unwind."

"I see. You aren't drinking. You don't drink?"

"I just got here. I like to get adjusted to everything before I have one. You know, the music, the darkness."

"Let me get your eyes adjusted. Say, let's take off that coat."

Johnny jerked and stopped her. The gun was in the right inside pocket. It was wrapped and well concealed. He didn't want Hershey to feel the weight of his jacket. The air conditioning was pumping at a good pace and Johnny did not feel the need to take off his jacket. He definitely did not want Hershey to touch it.

"Let me do it." He said. Johnny removed his jacket without giving a hint he was carrying anything inside his coat. Hershey and Johnny spoke for several minutes more. He did like the attention of another woman and enjoyed her personality. After discussing such topics of where he was from and what he liked, Hershey asked, "Well, would you like a dance?"

"Sounds like a great idea."

"Right here or a private room?"

"Right here is fine," he smiled.

Hershey went immediately into her gyrations. Her movements were different from Diamond's, but had the same results: pleasure. Johnny never saw Diamond walk into the club with her roller bag of outfits. She headed towards the dressing room and never noticed Johnny was being entertained. Once in the dressing room she went for her locker.

Baby saw Diamond and immediately came up to her. "Any luck?" she asked.

Diamond reach into her purse and pulled out two plastic sandwich bags.

"OK, here you go. You see I have put #1 on one bag and #2 on the other. Tomorrow, take the first pill, wait at least thirty minutes and take the next."

"You the best Diamond. Thank you. Something you need to know. A new girl here, black, she out there with your Johnny right now."

Diamond peered out the dressing room door and Baby pointed out where the action was taking place. Diamonds fingers opened out as if to reveal her claws. She looked at Baby, "Go out and bring her back here. I don't want to make a scene in front of Johnny"

The song ended, Hershey asked Johnny if he wanted her to go on. He shook his head and gave her a twenty. Baby walked over to the two of them smiled and looked up at Hershey. "Come back to dressing room please." Hershey continued to smile as she nodded her head. "I'll check back in with you later, ok?" Johnny nodded.

Back in the dressing room Diamond was ready to pounce. When Hershey entered, Diamond's demeanor was fierce. Her voice was violent, "I know you are new here, but I'm going to let you in on some ground rules. That man you were just with, he is off limits. He is mine. I've been working him for weeks. Hands off, do you understand?"

"Who the hell do you think you are? All these guys are up for grabs. I didn't see a sign on him. He didn't push me away or say sorry, I'm taken."

Listen, you bitch, stay away from him or you'll regret it."

Hershey stood still, her eyes and face still standing up to Diamond. She was not sure what Diamond was capable of and did not want to take any chances. "Ok, the old man is yours. I will spend my time with the young bucks. They seem to like younger girls." Hershey walked back on to the floor and immediately found another victim.

Diamond finished her clothes, makeup, then sprayed a spot of Armani on her neck while giving her hair one last toss before hitting the floor. She made her way to Johnny. He stood up when she approached and Diamond just shook her head and smiled. "Always the gentleman aren't you?"

"Always, for the ladies."

"Have you been here long?" Diamond pried.

"Maybe half an hour, I'm not sure."

"I hope you weren't bored sitting back here all by yourself." She continued to be subtle as she interrogated.

"No not at all. A new girl came over to keep me company. I thought of her as the warm up act, you know a prelude to the main event."

"I see." Diamond's manner seemed indifferent to what Johnny was saying.

"You are not jealous are you?" said Johnny.

"Of course not. You can see whoever you want. I just thought I was your girl." Her voice peaked a higher pitch.

"You are my girl." Johnny pulled closer to her. "Besides, I've got a surprise for you."

"What did you bring me hun?"

"Open your purse." Johnny reached into his coat pocket and pulled out an object covered with cloth that fit in the palm of his hand. He dropped it in her purse.

"Well, don't I get to see it?"

"No, not now, not here."

"What is it?" Diamond was curious and frightened at the same time. Johnny drew nearer to her and whispered, "It's a gun."

Diamond moved away; her face was startled. "You are kidding right?"

"No, it is for you, for your protection. Sneak it into your locker when you get a chance and then take it home.

"Alright, I have never had a gun before. By the way, I have something to ask you. It is about a customer who comes in here."

"I doubt I know any of the customers. I just sit by myself and talk to you."

"I think this one works at your company. His name is Cord."

Johnny was motionless. He felt the fantasy was fading and reality was setting in. "I know someone named Cord who works in my department. Why?"

"He got one of the girls here pregnant."

"No way, that is crazy. He is a family man with a wife and kids." Johnny was aghast.

"Yep, and that is what he told her. He also told her to get rid of it and he would pay."

"I don't believe it, not Cord."

"Well believe it. That is where you come in. The girl does not want to see Cord anymore but she needs the money he has promised."

"What do you want me to do?" Johnny was afraid, he didn't want to get involved in this mess.

"You are to talk with Cord. She wants $2000 for the operation, mental trauma and the emotional stress he has given her. Bring it to me here on Wednesday."

"I will talk to Cord and get to the bottom of this. Good night, I'll see you on Wednesday. I am not in the mood to be entertained right now. Johnny stood up and walked out of the club leaving Diamond alone at the table, without any tips, and a gun in her purse.

When Diamond got home, she put the gun away in her top dresser drawer under some lingerie. She had not made up her mind if having it was a good thing or not. She never had a gun before, but she felt a new sense of power come over her now that she had one. "I won't be taking crap from anyone," she thought out loud. She took the gun out of the drawer and held it in her hand. It had a nice fit. She spun around and pretended to shoot. "Pow! Bang!" she shouted. "You should have known better than to screw with me." She put the gun back in the drawer under her lingerie.

CHAPTER 19

——————●

BABY DIDN'T GET OUT OF BED until after noon on Sunday. Her sister Tran was working at the restaurant. Baby went for her purse on the nightstand. She took out the two pills Diamond had given her the night before. She went into the bathroom, filled a glass of water and without thinking, took both pills at once. Within an hour she began to feel cramps. She went into the bathroom and sat on the toilet as the pain intensified.

She could feel she was bleeding and something was coming out of her body. The cramps continued as did the bleeding. Baby became dizzy and disoriented. The room was spinning, her forehead was drenched in sweat. Her breathing became deep and heavy. She tried holding on to the tub nearby, but it was no use. She passed out toppling over the toilet. Her head made a cracking sound as it hit the tile floor. She lay on the floor bleeding and unconscious, unknown to anyone of the peril her life was in.

Tran came home at 9:00. It had been a busy shift. She had done well on her tips and she could not wait to soak her worn feet in a hot tub. The house was dark and there was no sign of Baby. Tran thought that interesting because her sister never left without turning on the outside light.

She called out her sister's name, "Hoa, Hoa?" but there was no answer. She went in the bedroom and took of her shoes and stockings. She headed towards the bathroom to start her bath. Upon opening the door, to her horror, she saw her little sister lying on the floor in a pool of blood with nothing but a short silk night shirt on.

Tran screamed, "Hoa, no, oh God no." She dropped to her knees and lifted Baby's head up and noticed the cut across her forehead smeared in blood. She felt for a pulse in Baby's neck, but there was none. She was gone. Tran sat in the blood and pulled Baby to her lap and cried.

A neighbor heard the screams and came running over to see the tragic scene. She called 911 though it was too late. The ambulance arrived in minutes. Tran rode with her sister to the hospital crying all the way.

On Monday, Johnny went into work early. He wasn't looking forward to the discussion he needed to have with Cord. He did not like confrontation. How should he approach the situation? He needed to know if Diamond had been honest with him or if it was a scam. Johnny wondered how he ever got mixed up in this cauldron of problems. He picked up his phone and called Cord's desk leaving a message on his machine directing him to come to his office as soon as possible.

At 8:30, Cord walked in Johnny's office. He gave Johnny a smile. "You wanted to see me?"

"Yes Cord, Close the door and have a seat."

"Wow serious. What's up?" Cord slouched into one of the office chairs.

"Yes it is, Cord. I don't know how to say this, so I'll get right to the point. Do you know an Asian girl who works at the Chase called Baby?"

Cord sat up straight in his chair. He could feel his throat go dry as he tried to swallow. What did Johnny know? How did he know? He took a deep breath and answered. "Sure, I know who she is, I have had a dance or two from her. Cute kid. What's the big deal?"

"Word has it you have had more than just a dance. I have been told she is pregnant with your child and you suggested she get an abortion." Johnny was leaning over his desk looking Cord square in the eye. Cord was frozen, his eyes glassy, "Johnny, you have to understand, it's not like you think."

"Tell me then Cord, how is it?"

"It was just supposed to be a game. You know two consenting adults having fun and then each going their own way. I thought since she was in that business she would be taking precautions, you know protection, maybe on the pill?" Cord put his right elbow up on the desk and leaned his head in his hand.

"I was contacted last night by someone at the club. The person who called me said Baby expects you to pay her $2000 for her operation and troubles. I'm expected to bring the money to the club Wednesday night."

"$2000? That is blackmail! What if I don't?" Cord smarted back.

"The person said they would call your wife and tell all. I will expect the money on Friday morning. I would recommend you not go back to the Chaise. Go back to your desk, we have got a project we are trying to save."

After Cord left, Johnny realized he had been spending too much money at the club. He decided a withdrawal from his 401K was in order rather than hit his savings just to keep things discrete. Only he knew how much he had invested. He submitted a withdrawal for $20,000.

Diamond showed up at the Chaise that night picking up one of Page's shifts. The opportunities were few and the atmosphere was grave. Sweets came over to her on her way to the dressing room. He stopped her and put his hand on her shoulder and said in his soft deep voice, "Come over here and sit down with me for a second."

"What's going on, you're so serious and sad." Diamond was curious about what was on Sweets' mind although her mood was unchanged.

"I don't know how to tell you this, you know Baby?" Sweets was stammering.

"Of course I do. I love the kid."

"She's dead Diamond. Her sister called me last night. Apparently she knew Baby worked here."

"That's impossible Sweets. I was with her Saturday night. How did it happen?" Diamond pretended to be in shock.

"From what I've been told it sounds like she was pregnant and it was a damm miscarriage gone wrong. Did you know she was pregnant?"

"I had no idea. She was so tiny, so young. I can't believe it."

"Ok now, I've already had words with the rest of the staff. Not a word to anyone. No one mentions this, understood?"

"I got ya boss. My lips are sealed. Is there a funeral or anything? Do we send flowers?"

"No. Her sister is taking her back to Viet Nam to be buried there. Me and a few friends are helping with the cost. Go get dressed. Remember, nothing has changed."

When Johnny arrived on Wednesday, he stopped at the bar before joining Diamond. "Scotch on the rocks, two shots to start, I'm thirsty. Also the usual for Diamond over there." Johnny picked up the drinks and joined Diamond, she was her old siren self. She was ready to play the game. She had the smile, and the look. She was ready for action, and Johnny was ripe for the picking, or so she thought.

"Oh I see you're a drinking man now. A little different from the shy boy I first met over two months ago."

"You know, I like a drink in my hand. I don't know, I think it makes me look like more of a man. What about you?"

"Johnny, I think you are all man." She kissed his cheek.

Diamond's charms were working like a snake charmer's pungi. She felt in control again. A couple more drinks and she would score once again with money man. They listened to the surround sound of pulsating beats the DJ was spinning while downing their drinks. The waitress came by spying their glasses nearly empty and Johnny said, "Let's do it again."

"Well you seem to be in a good mood tonight." Diamond tugged on Johnny's arm while he brushed her knee with his fingertips.

"I feel good. I think things are starting to fall into place for me." Diamond was not sure if it was the alcohol talking or the new Johnny. She was not sure how to work him. She had to adjust her tactics. Before she could get out another word, Johnny spoke up.

"I met with Cord today, I'll bring you the money on Friday. I just want to put this one to bed and forget about it"

"Thanks hun. Let's not talk any more about unpleasant things. Let's get some private time," she said as she lightly bit on Johnny's earlobe. Johnny waved a high sign to Sweets and pointed to the private room. Sweets nodded as Johnny escorted Diamond into their retreat of pleasure.

As they went into the room, Diamond realized neither Johnny nor Cord knew about Baby's death. Why would they? It certainly was not front page news and it was not like they were family. Diamond was the only one who knew of Baby's relationship with Cord, and she was not talking. Once in the private room, Diamond let Johnny take her in his arms and hold her while he kissed her neck. "This is going to be the easiest two grand I've ever made," she thought.

CHAPTER 20

O N FRIDAY MORNING, CORD WENT DIRECTLY to Johnny's office. He closed the door behind him. Johnny swiveled in his chair away from his computer and eyed Cord. Cord remained standing and reached into his inside coat pocket. He pulled out a white, bulging business sized envelope.

"Here you go; it's all there." He dropped the envelope on Johnny's desk. "This had better be the end of it. This is blackmail," Cord reiterated.

"I don't think so." Johnny picked up the envelope and locked it in his desk. "Let's just say payment for services rendered. A pretty expensive piece if I do say so. I hope it was worth it."

"Screw you." Cord stormed out of Johnny's office and went back to his desk.

Johnny worked in his office for the next few hours. He continued to go over and modify several charts related to the project. He had to give a presentation to Al Rogers later that afternoon. He wasn't looking forward to it. The X-Lab prototype delivery was a little more than a month away. Johnny had no progress to report and did not know how to put a positive spin on the negative status.

At 11:30, Ron Crocker appeared outside of Johnny's office door with a courtesy knock.

"Got a minute?"

"Sure, what's up?"

"I think I have some good news to offer."

"Great I need it, have a seat." Ron closed the door and pulled up a chair and sat down in front of Johnny. "You remember I asked Dana Pulley to look into the problems with the PDM?"

"Yeah, I remember. By the way I haven't seen much of her lately. Is she ok?"

"She's fine; she's been working from home and Joe Bordan is helping her."

"Alright, I know several folks telecommute."

"Anyway, she had a breakthrough. She had been running the PDM with the configuration test data, while modifying registry parameters at certain breakpoints. Bottom line, she has resolved several roadblocks that were crashing the software."

Johnny's eyes lit up. "You mean she's solved the problem?"

"No, not yet, but she is close. Nobody knows about this. She and Joe have more testing to do. We are keeping quiet about this, only the four of us are aware. We do not want to mention this to the other employees yet. It will just stir up rumor and false hope."

"Understood."

"I am telling you Johnny, I think she is going to do it."

Johnny clapped his hands together and slid his chair away from his desk. He was all smiles. "That is great news. If you are right about this, it will save our butts."

"You are going to see Big Al this afternoon, right?"

"Yep, we're on for 2:00"

"Great. You can let Al know we have made significant progress but you do not want to bore him with all the technical details. Go ahead and create some charts that show we are back on track."

"Are we back on track?"

"It's hard to say. *It depends* is the best answer I can give right now. If we meet the deadline we will be heroes, if not we will be polishing our resumes." Ron coughed as he was laughing.

"Thanks pal, I can definitely work this up. I'll get Paul Miller to put a presentation together. Give my thanks and appreciation to Dana. Let her know if she needs anything, I will get it for her."

"She has everything she needs at home. She says her setup is much more sophisticated than we have. I do know she built her own private network with impenetrable firewalls. She is a pretty sharp gal."

"Yeah, smart but dangerous." They both laughed.

"Good luck this afternoon. Oh by the way, how are things working out for your friend at the apartment? All settled in?"

"He is still getting adjusted, but he is much better off than he was before. Thanks again." Ron smiled and nodded as he left Johnny's office. Johnny picked up his phone and called Paul Miller. "Paul, come into my office. I have something I need you to put together for me ASAP."

Paul Miller, a gifted technician, was known as the spin doctor. He chose to make use of his intellectual talents by creating situations where he seemed totally indispensable, yet never delivered anything tangible.

He was always busy in a meeting or developing charts that no one understood or cared about due to their complexity and ambiguity. Paul had once remarked during a performance appraisal that if he were a manager, he would give anything to have an employee like himself.

Paul could have been at the senior technician level had he used his time producing earned value for the company rather than boasting how valuable he was. Paul was not lazy, quite the opposite. He worked hard creating colorful bullshit that could speak for hours without saying anything.

Johnny radiated confidence as he walked into Al Rogers' office. He connected his laptop to the mini technical media center that existed there. Paul Miller had once again worked his magic. The presentation was a tapestry of high definition graphics, spreadsheets and numerous charts full of an eye pleasing buzz that resembled nothing more than a cubic zirconia wrapped in a gold band.

Rogers was impressed and commended Johnny for the great work and progress. Johnny reminded Rogers that they were not announcing their progress until they solved the problem. Rogers agreed that was a good idea.

That evening, Johnny appeared to be in his best mood in weeks. He was cordial and spoke pleasantly with Jenny. He smiled at her, complimented her on the dinner and kissed her on the cheek. Jenny wondered why the sudden change, but was not about to ask. Johnny carried his dishes into the kitchen and said, "Things are looking up at work. We might actually deliver on time."

"Oh Johnny, that's wonderful." Jenny smiled wide eyed.

"Well, we are not out of the woods yet, but at least now it is progressing." Johnny rinsed his dishes in the sink. "The boys and I are planning on doing a little celebrating at the club tonight if that if you don't mind."

"That's fine, I didn't have any plans for us." Jenny was not about to ruin his mood. She was ecstatic seeing her husband cheerful like he used to be. She did not care where he was going. She would let him go and do whatever he wanted as long as he remained jubilant.

Johnny left the house around 8:30. He wanted to get a couple drinks under his belt and unwind before Diamond arrived. He was on a high, nothing could set him off, not even hitting every red light on the way to the Chaise.

Johnny was a block away from the Chaise as he sat at another red light. He did not notice the grey sedan behind him. The driver of the sedan immediately recognized the Mustang and her father. Maddy was behind him.

"What was he doing down here at this time of night?" She thought. Maddy had just finished shopping at the mall and was taking the side streets home. She was about to tap the horn to get her father's attention when the light turned green. Johnny moved into the left hand lane and turned left instead of heading home. As Maddy continued on, her eyes glanced to the left and saw the lights of The Chaise.

When Maddy got home, she brought in her bags and called out. "Jim, Jim, come here."

"What's the matter babe? You alright?"

"I don't know. You can't believe what I just saw."

"What, what did you see?"

"I saw my dad drive over to the strip club!" There was anxiety in her voice.

"What? You're joking. Are you sure?"

"I know my dad's car and I saw him. I was right behind him."

"Did he see you?"

"No, I'm sure he had other things on his mind." She responded sarcastically.

Jim took a hold of Maddy's hands. He spoke slowly as he tried to calm her down. Maddy was still upset. She was starting to shake and was not listening to Jim. "Why would he be going there? I talk with mom almost every other day. She has never mentioned a problem. What do you think is going on?"

Jim spoke up, "You don't know what's going on. There may be a good reason." Before he could finish Maddy opened up, "Yeah, what good reason? What kind of a reason does a middle-aged, happily married man need to watch a bunch of young women dance naked?"

"You're jumping to conclusions. Did you see him go in?"

"No, I kept driving. There is nowhere else to go except that parking lot. It's a dead end!"

"Maybe he was just trying to turn around, you know make a U-turn."

"No, I looked in the rearview mirror. I never saw him coming out. Are you siding with him, defending him? You men are all the same, you stick together no matter what."

"Now wait a minute, I am not siding with or defending anyone. All I am saying is we do not know what's going on. You know, things are not always what they seem."

Maddy went towards the phone in the kitchen. "I'm calling mom. I'm going to find out what's going on. Maybe they had a big fight. Maybe she needs me."

"Stop right there, you are not calling your mom." Jim took the receiver out of Maddy's hand. "If your mom needed you, she would have called. Whatever is going on, it is none of our business. This is your parents' business. If they want to bring us in, they will. Jim put the receiver back on the phone and Maddy went into the bedroom crying.

By the time Diamond made her way through the entrance of the Chaise, Johnny had already downed two scotch on the rocks. He was really beginning to develop a taste for scotch and was now experimenting with the higher quality brands such as Caskers, Gleniddich, and Balvenie. Johnnie Walker Red wasn't good enough anymore; it had to be Blue Label. As Johnny's taste went up so did the price. His drinks were no longer $5-$7; they soared upward to $15-$25. Johnny had been keeping track of the money he spent at the Chaise over the last two months, it came to almost $4000. But Johnny wasn't worried about the cost. He felt he could afford it and he thought it made him look important. Besides, he knew he had another $20,000 coming in from his 401K.

Diamond came out in a red, floral embroidered, sheer body suit that left nothing to the imagination. A silk, white lace, shawl covered her shoulders. She strutted over to Johnny in her three-inch red stilettoes.

"Hi, hun," she winked. "I hope I haven't kept you waiting long."

"Not at all. I've just been loosening up, shall we say. It's been a good day, I'm all relaxed and you are my night-cap."

"Oh Johnny, you are so cute."

Johnny, reached into his jacket pocket and pulled out the envelop Cord had brought him. "Here, put this in your purse and lock it up." Diamond took the money and put it in her purse. She leaned closer to Johnny and whispered, "Now that the business is out of the way, what shall we do?"

Johnny grinned, "I think all the privates are empty, why don't we get one?" Johnny walked over to Sweets near the bar and pushed a handful of cash into his open palm. Sweets smiled, "Take your pick, they're all open."

Johnny took Diamond by the hand. She embraced his right arm while holding his hand in between hers. Johnny slid the curtain just enough for them to pass into the room. He sat himself down on the brown leather couch. The DJ's beat worked in rhythm to Diamond's erotic enticing. She kicked off her stilettoes and let the draped kimono slide down her arms onto the floor. Her arms crossed her breast as her finger tips slid under the spaghetti straps of her body suit revealing all that God had given her. She moved closer to Johnny and put one knee on his thigh and rubbed her cheek on his while blowing in his ear. Johnny drew his face to hers, kissed her on the lips and said, "I love you Diamond."

CHAPTER 21

THREE MONTHS HAD PASSED SINCE JOHNNY first made his way through the velvet curtains of the Chaise lounge. He could be seen there on a Wednesday, Friday or Saturday. He would attend at least once or twice a week depending on his mood. He became a familiar personage along with his main stay Diamond.

Johnny spent most of his time with Diamond, but occasionally he would indulge himself and allow his ego to be stroked by a different girl before Diamond arrived. Johnny relished his new found popularity where his confidence emerged. His appearance was relaxed. He developed flirtatious remarks as he was becoming more of a gamer. Johnny bought drinks for the Chaise ladies who in turn reciprocated with suggestive, playful innuendos.

The Chaise was a new found drug for Johnny. It was a euphoric delight enhanced with beautiful women, pulsating rhythms, and alcohol. But like all drugs, the illusion would come to a harsh end with the arrival of reality. Each ensuing, intoxicating fantasy was met with a resounding crash once the titillating elixir of devoted feminine pleasure had come to an end. Reality replaced rapture with melancholy. It was as though Johnny was on auto pilot at 35,000 feet only to lose all engines and crash dive into the abyss of depression once the drug wore off. Johnny was living in two different worlds. One was a lie, combining fantasy with emotional ecstasy, the other was a void known as the truth, a sordid dark place that included a job, home and a wife who couldn't make him happy.

Johnny's emotional persona was not the only victim, his physical appearance at work also took a decline. No longer were the definitions of impeccable dress the defining hallmarks of Johnny's character. His coordination of shirts, slacks and shoes were now irrelevant, so was his grooming. He only shaved a few times a week leaving his face with a small stubble. His hair was often disheveled or so heavily laden with product it appeared to need an oil change. He had become a dark, sullen figure whose cold eyes were void of sentiment when he went to work every day. There was a short fuse attached to his mood and the slightest provocation could ignite it. Of course all of that would change on a Wednesday, Friday or Saturday night. Johnny cleaned up properly and dressed well whenever he went to the Chaise. His thoughts were only on his shameless obsession: Diamond.

Johnny had not been sleeping well. He would lie in a state of restlessness for several hours before he would help himself to his hidden stock of white rum and scotch. This solution aided him in times of insomnia. Johnny slept alone in the guest room which had now become his sanctuary. When Johnny awoke that Friday, his eyes were tired with the small red veins pronounced. There was the slight scent of alcohol following him although he was not drunk.

He spent little time prepping for work. A wet wash cloth around his face and other parts of his body, along with deodorant, was all the personal hygiene Johnny required.

Johnny arrived at work around 8:15 am. First item of business was to get the coffee started, He was not overly concerned with promptness but understood the importance of a professional work ethic at RayCom, as well as the value of a paycheck. He continued to feed his habit at the Chaise and while playing the extravagant suitor to Diamond. Diamond always had a story for Johnny and he would always reprise his role as the benevolent knight in shining armor obliging her request. Besides the withdrawal from his 401K, Johnny was close to maxing one of his credit cards. He deceived himself thinking that he would start paying it back once he regained control of his finances. Just as the spring rain evaporates from the sidewalk, Johnny's disposable funds were beginning to drying up.

Johnny powered up his computer and checked his calendar. There were a number of meetings scheduled he felt were either useless, irrelevant or did not merit his offering an opinion. There was one however he was interested in, the technical team status of the X-Lab prototype.

The project was 2 months behind schedule. RayCom was in jeopardy of losing a five million dollar contract. Johnny thought, "How could that still be the case? ProSoft guaranteed the problems would be resolve in the next release, but that would be too late. To make matters worse, the vendor's product was in the middle of contract negotiations."

Johnny envisioned a plaque of shame outside his office with the names and photos of the five managers who failed. Johnny saw his name and photo gracing the plaque. While Johnny pondered this disturbing dilemma, Ron Crocker knocked on his door.

Ron Crocker greeted Johnny. "Good morning. Busy?"

"No, come in." Johnny answered.

"You look like Hell!" Ron observed.

"I didn't sleep well last night. I've got a lot on my mind."

"Well, you will like the sound of this. I think Dana Pulley and Joe Bordan have a solution to our X-Lab problems. Looks like it could be a bug in the vendor software."

Johnny's eyes lit up like headlights. "That's great, this will save our butts. What did they do?"

"I do not know exactly. Dana gave me very vague details. She seemed confident that she and Joe have discovered the problem."

"Send her in. I want to thank her and talk with her about it."

"You got it chief." Ron headed out to the cubicle bay where Dana was working. "Hey Dana, I just gave Johnny the good news and he wants to congratulate you."

"You what?" Dana exclaimed. "Why on earth did you do that?"

"I figured you were going to let him know at the status meeting today, I wanted to give him a heads up. What's the problem?"

"I'm not ready to make it public. Joe and I still have more work to do"

"But I thought it works and you put it into production." Ron quizzed

"That's true. I have it in the production system that I imported to my home computer, not here at work. There are reasons no one should know about this yet. Thanks for nothing."

Dana headed over to Johnny's office. She was angry. She was sure Johnny would be upset at her methods and not realize she only had the company's best interest with the path she chose. She walked at a slower pace as she approached Johnny's open door.

"Dana, sit down and tell me all about it, I just heard the good news."

"Not much to tell right now, still in testing, gathering results", she was elusive.

"Nonsense, this is a big deal. What did you do to fix the software? I had no idea you were close to a solution." Johnny was beaming, "Tell me he more."

"Well if you must know, here is the short answer. Joe Bordan and I worked with the supplier on his code. It was pretty complex but after a few weeks, working on it together at my house, we developed several new algorithms and created a patch for the vendor's software. We tested it and we deployed it into production."

"I'm not sure I follow you?" Johnny's expression was slowly twisting.

"The supplier has allowed us to use a beta test of their software at my house and access to their source. I also uploaded the product data we had generated for X-Lab and ran it through a debugger I have. Joe discovered several parameters were exceeding thresholds and crashing the software. Once we identified them, we worked with the supplier to modify the code and fix the bugs."

Johnny's voice increased in volume. "Do you realize what you two have done?"

"Yes, we have ensured RayCom will deliver the prototype on time and win the contract and we will keep our jobs." Snapped Dana

"No you haven't. You have put us in a compromising, unethical position. Not only is this unethical, it is probably illegal. You have worked on a vendor product that you had no authority to, on a version we have no license for, and put into production without going through the proper software deployment process with our security folks. All of this while we are in contract negotiations with the supplier. You have opened a Pandora's Box of scandals for our company. Get out of my office while I think of the best way to handle this."

"That's your problem. All management ever does is think about the bottom line and reputation. I'm a technician. I take action, I develop solutions. I do the work that needs to be done that others are afraid to do. You are always content with the results when you don't know how you got them but go flying off the handle once you learn the truth. You stick your precious reputation up your ass. I did my part." Dana stood up and shoved her chair against Johnny's desk and stormed out of his office.

Johnny raised his elbows up on desk and clasped his hands and tucked his thumbs under his chin. He never imagined a situation like this. The technical problems of the X-Lab project were solved, but at what cost? Johnny knew he had to go forward and deliver the prototype. He knew he was compromising his standards. He envisioned a cover-up knowing sooner or later the truth would come percolating out.

Cord happened to be walking by Johnny's office while Dana and Johnny were exchanging words. He stood to the side of the door and listened. Cord seized opportunity. He went upstairs to Al Rogers' office and told him what he had heard.

"As bad as this sounds Al, I think I have a solution that will work for everyone. I have a connection in the executive offices at ProSoft and he is a pretty reasonable guy. You and I both know that neither company wants a scandal, nor can either of us afford one. Let me get in touch with him see what can work out."

Al Rogers listened to Cord with serious concern. "Cord, we are going forward with the prototype and we are going to deliver on time. You work with your connection at ProSoft and make this right. I am counting on you Cord, do not let me down."

CHAPTER 22

WITHIN MINUTES OF DANA LEAVING JOHNNY'S office, his phone rang. It was Al Rogers.

"Johnny, I've just been apprised of the X-Lab situation and possible ethical implications." Johnny took a deep breath, he felt that his heart had stopped. He spoke slowly and calmly. "But how…? I just now found out myself. Does everyone else know and I'm last on the list?"

"No, Cord updated me and he has a plan to make this go away. I don't want you to worry. There are only a few of us who know and nobody is talking. We are going ahead as planned and we will meet our target. You call a staff meeting for later this afternoon. Recognize Dana Pulley as the one who solved the problem and give her an instant appreciation award. You know, a 'Night on the Town' thing. Thank everyone for a job well done and leave it at that."

There was a sick feeling in the pit of Johnny's stomach. He had just finished chastising Dana, now he had to swallow his pride, go against his principles and reward her. Then the irony of the situation caused him to chuckle, Johnny understood, business was business and he would do as he was told.

That afternoon Johnny had all the employees associated with the X-Lab project convene in a large conference room. Johnny took his spot at the far end of the conference table and got everyone's attention. "Good afternoon. I'm not going to bore you folks with a plethora of slides that would guarantee an end to insomnia. I'll get right to it. I have good news. Thanks to the incredible efforts of one of your peers, the X-Lab project is back on track, the configuration management issue in the PDM has been resolved, and we are going to meet our schedule and deliverable for the prototype." There were cheers, applause, and whisperings while Johnny spoke.

"It gives me great pleasure to award this 'Night on the Town' to Dana Pulley." The applause and cheers intensified. "She has worked countless, unreported hours from her home, working with a vendor through endless testing and coding until she discovered and resolved the problem. Dana, I want to thank you personally for what may be saving the future of RayCom, not to mention saving my butt as well. Dana, come on up."

Johnny held an envelope in his hand with a certificate for Dana. He handed it to her and shook her hand. The employees were on their feet cheering and talking. It was a sight of great joy. Dana raised her hand to quiet the staff down. "I want to let you all know I did not do this alone. Joe Bordan was with me all the way and I plan on sharing this award with him. Also, thanks to all of you who kept feeding us great test data which allowed us to narrow down several problems. I want to thank everyone here, it was a team effort." The staff applauded once more.

Johnny stood up and took over. "That's it gang, everyone back to work, there is still plenty of work to be done. Dana will get you all set up with the software modifications she developed and you can go from there." Dana stayed in the conference room with Johnny after the group had been dismissed.

"Thanks boss, I can only imagine how hard that was for you." She had the sneer of success.

"Don't thank me." Johnny grimaced, "It was the chief's idea."

Johnny hated the charade he was forced to play. He went back into his office and closed the door behind him. He sat down at his desk and opened his bottom drawer on the right side. His friend Johnnie Walker was staring up at him. Johnny pulled out a shot glass and downed it as quickly as he poured it. There was a knock on his door. Johnny immediately put the bottle and shot glass back in the drawer. As he closed the drawer, he called out, "Come in."

It was Ron Crocker. "That was some show my friend. They needed a morale boost and you gave it to them. They are energized my friend, and I believe we will hit our target."

"Don't thank me, it was Al's idea. I had already bawled Dana out for creating a possible ethics issue."

"What are you talking about?"

"You mean to say you don't know how she accomplished this?"

"Sure. A lot of hard work, day after day, night after night."

"Whew," Johnny sighed. "I feel a whole lot better now knowing you were just as much in the dark as I was. I'll give Dana credit, she did put in a lot of hard work, but she compromised us. She crawled in the sheets with ProSoft utilizing unauthorized software." Ron was in shock.

"I had no idea. What are we going to do?"

"Cord went to Al with a plan. Apparently he has some connections at ProSoft. They seem to think the ethical issues can be worked out between the two companies legally. Al told me not to worry, you know business as usual."

"I guess we really are just pawns in the game." Johnny asked Ron to close the door and sit down. "I've got something to tell you Ron. I'm about to bust and I need to tell someone. You're the only one I can tell. Not a word to anyone."

"You got it man. What's going on?"

"I'm leaving Jenny. I have found someone else." Ron thought his jaw had just hit the floor. He couldn't believe what he just heard.

"What? You can't mean that!"

"It's true Ron. I do not even believe it myself, but it's true. In fact, I have you to thank for it." Ron was totally confused.

"What are you talking about? I had nothing to do with this." Ron was getting angry.

"You're the one who got me out to the gentlemen's club three months ago. I met her there."

"A stripper? Oh come on, the jokes over, you're kidding me right?"

"No Ron, I've been seeing her a couple of times a week and we're in love."

"But what about Jenny? Maddy, the boys?"

"I will see that they are taken care of. I have already got the divorce papers filled out. Look at this." Johnny pulled out a ring box from the middle top drawer of his desk. Johnny opened the box and proudly displayed the fourteen carat gold solitaire with a one carat diamond.

"Are you out of your mind? You can't possibly be serious."

"I am. Diamond loves me and we're going to be married." Johnny spoke sternly as he stood up. Ron came over to the side of the desk face to face with Johnny.

"Diamond, no way! Johnny she's a con. I don't know what she has said to you, but she is playing you."

"You are wrong Ron. We have got something. We have both felt it. I got her set up in the apartment I rented from you and I am going to move in until we can get another place."

"She is your down and out friend? I have heard everything. I do not believe this."

Johnny put out his hands in front of Ron gesturing him to calm down. "I did not like lying to you, but I had to, because I knew you would not approve."

"You're damm right I wouldn't." There was as increase of volume in Ron's voice as he spoke. "Johnny she's playing you, I can understand the sexual attraction and whatever intimate offerings she's given you, but I know she is not the marrying kind."

"How dare you insinuate that I am having an affair! Ours is not that kind of relationship. We don't need sex to know we are in love."

"Let me get this straight, you don't know her real name, you haven't screwed her, you continue to give her money, and yet you want me to believe she is willing to marry you. Don't be a fool Johnny." A few employees began to gather near Johnny's office to see what the commotion was.

"I've heard enough. I thought you were my friend and would understand."

"I'm not done, but since you are lost in your dream, I'll let you know how things really are. I hate to burst your bubble pal, but she's a whore. When she's not working the club she's turning tricks. How do I know this? Because I have been doing her for months. What is crazier, is heaven only knows how much you have spent on her without getting laid. You have got to be the dumbest fu…"

Before Ron could finish he found himself on the floor, an unexpected right-cross to the jaw came from nowhere, cutting his lip and dropping him to the floor.

"I will not hear you talk about her like that. You're a jealous liar." Ron sat on the floor beside Johnny's desk licking his lip. "You crazy son of a bitch" Al Rogers made his way into the office.

"What the hell is going on here?" he growled. Al looked at everyone outside of the office and said, "Everyone, get back to your desks. I'll deal with this. Ron are you OK?"

"Yeah, I think so." Ron put his chin in his hand as he worked his jaw.

Al held out his hand and helped Ron up. "Go clean yourself up and go home. We'll talk about this later." Ron left the office and went down the hall to the men's room. There was disappointment in Al's eyes as he looked down at Johnny. "Now what was all this about?"

"Just a personal problem between Ron and me. I lost it, I'm sorry."

"Well I am going to see that the both of you get some counseling. We cannot tolerate this kind of behavior at the office. You two still have to work together as long one of you isn't fired. I have to submit a report to HR."

"I know," said Johnny as he pulled a large envelope from his desk drawer and handed it to Al.

"What this?" Al felt uneasy as he took the envelope from Johnny.

"It's my retirement papers. They are all filled in except for when the retirement date is to commence. I will leave that to you to fill in whatever date you feel appropriate. I am going home."

"Take a couple of days off as well," Al disciplined, "You need it."

With that Johnny walked out of his office leaving Al Rogers shaking his head and holding Johnny's retirement papers in his hand.

CHAPTER 23

MADDY COULD NOT STAND IT ANY longer, she needed to tell her mother about seeing Johnny driving over to the Chaise. The boys were at school so she drove out to her parent's home at 10:00. When Maddy arrived, Jenny was ecstatic to see her.

"I know it has only been a few days, but I'm glad you came by. Coffee?"

"Oh yes mom, and it does seem like forever since it has just been the two of us. We never get our time anymore, the boys, dad or Jim are always around, you know. I thought it would great just us girls today." Maddy giggled.

"Yes, we occasionally need time together without distractions."

"What? My boys are a distraction?" They both laugh. Maddy quieted down and with a thoughtful voice asked, "Is everything alright with you and dad?"

"Why of course," Jenny immediately responded. "Why would you ask that?"

"Well I never see dad anymore. He is always gone whenever I come over. I know a lot of times I come over while he is working, but when I come by later in the evening, he is either gone or in his back office working. Lately he has not even come out to say hi when I am here. It makes me wonder."

"Your father has been under a lot of pressure at work. This new project is really getting to him. I don't know anything about it. Your father says I wouldn't understand and he is right. He is worried about losing his job if things do not go well with this project and he is considering retirement. A few times he has been short with me, but I know it is the job. I do worry that he has been drinking lately to help him relax and unwind."

"He's been drinking? Did he get violent? Did he hit you mom?"

"Of course not. He just been down on himself and a bit negative lately, that's all."

"Mom, I don't know how to tell you this, but I saw something about a month ago and I am not sure what it means. Jim told me there is a reasonable explanation for it so maybe you can tell me." Maddy had caught her mother's interest.

"Well go on, tell me."

"Mom, I saw dad go into that club, the Chaise about a month ago, when I had finished shopping at the mall."

"I don't know anything about any club. What kind of place is it? A sports bar?"

"No, it is a strip club mom. Women dance practically naked on a stage and men toss money at them, I can't believe you haven't heard of it." Maddy was getting agitated at her mom's naivety. Jenny sat there silent for a minute not knowing what to say after hearing her daughter's words. An earthquake had shaken her sensitive heart.

"I guess he could be going there. He goes out once or twice a week. I don't know where he goes." A small pocket of tears arose in Jenny's eyes. She couldn't understand what was happening right now. Was Maddy right? Was Johnny seeing someone? Was their marriage falling apart? Jenny felt she had been a good wife, she let Johnny do whatever he wanted. She never put him down or questioned his decisions. Jenny sat in front of Maddy as if in a trance. She looked around the kitchen and her head turned towards the living room. Everything was in its place, neat and tidy. She tried to imagine what she had done wrong. She kept the house clean, cooked his meals, and did his laundry. She never nagged and was always positive with Johnny even when she disagreed with him. She always let him get his way and made it look like they both compromised. When it came to intimacy, she never refused him, and it didn't matter if she was in the mood or not. She felt that was part of her wifely duties.

"Mom?" Maddy tried to bring Jenny back to the conversation. "Mom are you still with me?" Jenny looked at Maddy and widened her eyes as if awakening from a bad dream,

"Yes, I'm here. I just don't know what to think or say."

"Are you guys having money problems?"

"Oh no, we talked about that the other day. Everything is fine financially."

"I think you and dad need to talk about this. It's better to get these things out in the open early before they fester and blow up in your face. Maybe you guys should think about a marriage counselor. I have to go home, the boys will be home from school soon. Talk to dad, call me if you need me."

Johnny walked through the door at 3:30. His demeanor was dark. He was brooding as he closed the door behind him. Jenny came out of the laundry room and saw Johnny standing in the hallway. She stopped after taking a few steps, she knew something was wrong. Johnny never came home this early and his features were frightening.

"What a nice surprise. You are home early. What's the occasion?" It was everything she could do to muster a smile as she spoke.

"Some occasion," he said sarcastically. "I was almost fired today, that's the special occasion."

"Oh Johnny dear, what happened, is it that project you are so worried about?"

"Yes, it's the project alright. I was discussing the project with Ron and the next thing I knew we were arguing and I punched him. I lost it, I hit my best friend." Jenny walked over to him and took his hand, "Oh Johnny, I'm so sorry".

"Here's the ironic twist, it comes when this should have been one of the best days at work ever. One of the employees solved the software problems and the project will in all likelihood be delivered on time. I just can't believe I lost it there at work. I don't even know who I am anymore."

All of the words Ron spoke were still incinerating inside him. Had he really been played for a fool? Was he just another mark who had been conned? Was Diamond more than an exotic dancer at a strip club? Was she a prostitute as Ron had suggested? Johnny needed the answers to all of these questions. He would go to the Chaise tonight, he would give Diamond the ring once he was alone with her. If she accepted, it didn't matter what Ron had said. If she declined, then he knew Ron was right. He looked at Jenny and said, "I need a drink."

"OK, do you want a beer? I bought some."

"No, thanks, I have something in the office. I am going to listen to my music. I could really use some opera right now." Johnny went into his office and poured himself a scotch. He began listening to the beautiful, yet tragically romantic arias of La Boheme. Within minutes, whether due to alcohol, fatigue or the day's events, Johnny was asleep.

When he awoke, several hours later, he was hungry. He went into the kitchen and opened the refrigerator. Jenny was watching television in the front room and called out, "What are you looking for?"

"I'm looking for something to eat." Johnny replied in a loud voice. He was not angry, he just wanted to make sure Jenny heard him. "What did you fix for dinner?"

"Nothing, I just made myself a salad and had some string cheese. That is all I was in the mood for. Would you like me to fix you something?"

"Sure, I know it sounds crazy, but I want a fried egg sandwich. Would you mind fixing one for me while I go clean up?"

"I don't mind, that's easy." Johnny went into the master bathroom and eyed his two day growth in the mirror. His slicked back hair was also in need of attention. He stood over the sink lathering his face then pulled the razor over his grisly stubble. He did not have much of a beard and if he were to let it grow out, it would be sparse and patchy. Up until the last month, he had always been clean shaven.

He didn't stay in the shower long, he was never known for long showers. He worked the wash cloth and soap over his body quickly and then washed his hair. By the time he dried off, put on deodorant and combed his hair, fifteen minutes had passed.

He came downstairs dressed casual but sharp. His khaki slacks and blue chino shirt were pressed with stiff creases. His tan crew socks and burgundy tasseled loafers completed the look he was after. He grabbed his tweed sport coat with suede elbow patches out of the closet. Once downstairs, he draped it over the back of his dining room chair. Jenny brought him his sandwich.

"Anything else? Would you like something to drink?"

"Yeah, I'll take that beer now. No need to pour it into a glass, just bring me the bottle." Jenny obliged. Johnny wasted no time in putting down his sandwich. He emptied the bottle of beer in four gulps. "Thank you dear, I'm off to the club. Don't wait up for me."

Jenny thought about what Maddy had told her earlier, she wanted to confront Johnny, but she was afraid of what his reaction might be, He was in a good mood now and she him to remain that way.

"Drive carefully," she said. And with that Johnny was out the door.

It was after 10:00 when Johnny arrived at the Chaise. The parking lot was full and so was the club. Johnny walked into what he deemed organized chaos. The thunderous sound reverberated through Johnny's body as he desperately tried to find a place to sit down or catch a glimpse of Diamond. All around him the sparsely attired dancers were warming men's laps in chairs that were meant to only accommodate one. There were three waitresses working the floor and two at the bar. Private rooms were occupied and there were few tables available. Johnny found a table near the stage and claimed it as though he had been riding in the Oklahoma land rush. He hated sitting so close to the action. He was not comfortable with the fact he was easily observed by the other patrons, but he felt obligated to toss dollar bills up there regardless of whether or not his impressions about the dancer were positive. Diamond spied Johnny from a table where she was entertaining. Johnny hadn't seen her and always had trouble spotting her when there was a large crowd. He sat patiently knowing Diamond would find him sooner or later.

Diamond's client was satisfied with two dances and paid her off. She thanked him and said she would check in on him later if he looked in need of company. She grabbed her purse and made her way over to Johnny's table.

"Hi hun, I didn't know if you were coming. It's crazy tonight. You doing ok?"

"I am now, it was a difficult day." Diamond patted the top of his wrist sympathetically.

"Let's say we start off with a couple of drinks and you tell me all about it."

Johnny flagged down a waitress and put in their usual order. With the Chaise so crowded, the temperature was steaming, the air conditioning couldn't keep up with all the bodies. Johnny removed his jacket. Johnny recapped the events of the day, (leaving out the confrontation he had with Ron) and portrayed himself as an innocent victim in, as what he called it, a "Comedy of Terrors".

"Oh you poor baby. That's the way it always is. The guilty ones always get away with their crap, and then the good guys, like you, are left holding the bag and take the blame."

"Are any of the privates available? I have something for you." Diamond surveyed the back area away from the bar. "Yes, there are two open. Go let Sweets know." Johnny picked up his jacket. He found Sweets and handed him $250. "How about thirty, will you let me have it?"

"I'm not supposed to, you know how it works." He paused, "Hmm, I tell you, I'm going let you have it this time because you are such a good customer and a good guy. Don't you go expecting it now. Mind you, if you take advantage of my good nature, you'll be looking for entertainment at another club." Johnny thanked him and went to the room where Diamond was waiting.

"I'm so excited, you brought me something. You are just so good to me Johnny, why?

Johnny looked into her eyes with admiration, "I thought I made that clear the other night." Diamond didn't want to go near the subject of love, she did her best to change the subject. "We do have a good times together here don't we Johnny?"

"Yes we do and that is what I want to talk to you about. I want us to keep on having these good times."

"And we will, every Wednesday, Friday and Saturday night." Diamond snickered to herself and thought herself smart and witty.

"You are right, but seriously, I do have something for you and I hope you will accept it."

"Well come on hun, I'm dying to see what you brought me." Johnny reached into his jacket's front pocket. He held the ring box inside his fist. He released his fist and with his left hand opened the box. Diamond's eyes began to roll from their sockets. The game had gone too far. She was not prepared for this.

Johnny then got down on one knee as he held the ring up to Diamond who sat frozen. He spoke gently. "Diamond, would you do me the honor of becoming my wife?" Johnny handed the ring to Diamond. She held it up and couldn't stop looking at it. She looked at Johnny and then again at the ring. She searched for words but nothing came to her. Finally she held Johnny's hand and replied. "Johnny it's beautiful. You shouldn't have."

"Is that a no?"

"No, well this is unexpected. No one has ever proposed to me before. I don't know what to say." She continued admiring the ring. "I'm flattered and a bit confused. I didn't realize you felt that way. When you told me you loved me, I thought it was just something to be said in the heat of the moment." Diamond was trying to regain control, it was not a game anymore. She knew she could not tell him no. She could feel the hook slipping out.

"Can you give me a couple of days to think about it?" Diamond needed to buy time.

"Yes, keep the ring for now and think about it. I'll come back tomorrow night for your answer. How's that?"

"OK, tomorrow night. I'll see you tomorrow night and give you my answer." There was a knock outside the private room door. Sweets authoritative deep voice resonated, "That's thirty."

CHAPTER 24

S ATURDAY MORNING BEGAN AS USUAL. JENNY was in the kitchen getting the coffee started and opened the fridge pulling out bacon and eggs. As Johnny came into the kitchen his senses were aroused by the aroma of the fresh coffee brewing. He looked completely relaxed in his tan shorts, topsiders and faded opera t-shirt he picked up at the Music Center years ago.

"You up for some breakfast dear? I've got plenty of eggs and a pound of bacon I need to cook."

"No thanks, just coffee and toast for me. Ah, maybe a couple of pieces of bacon. That sounds good. I'm going to do the lawns this morning while it's cool." Johnny went outside to bring in his newspaper and get a feel for the weather.

Johnny sat down at the table with his newspaper in hand, Jenny brought him his toast, more coffee and three strips of bacon. Johnny glanced at the front page. The Ebola epidemic in West Africa now seemed contained. There were border conflicts between Russia and the Ukraine which reminded Johnny of the Cold War in the sixties. There was fighting along the Gaza strip and al Qaeda, that was always in the news. The market was stable, which interested Johnny the most since he was considering retirement. He folded the paper and placed it where Jenny would sit, then took another sip of his coffee and kept his thoughts to himself.

The dry LA weather took out its wrath on Johnny's lawn. There was little rain that year in Southern California and residents had been asked to conserve water. Johnny watered the lawn sparingly and it showed. There were brown spots and dust patches mingled in with the green

Bermuda. Johnny's mower bounced over the uneven ranges as if it were a joyriding ATV. The lawn had seen better days. Nevertheless, it was still alive, growing, and needed to be cut.

Johnny had both the front and the back lawns finished in forty-five minutes. He went inside and called out, "I'm going to shower." He made no effort to find Jenny and went straight to the bathroom.

The shower refreshed Johnny. He dressed and headed to the back yard with a copy of David McCullough's 'John Adams' in hand. He loved historical biographies. His favorite was 'The Greatest Generation' by Tom Brokaw. He sat down in his lawn chair and took in the scent of the recently cut grass. The sun warmed his body as he began to read.

Jenny watched Johnny come back into the house in the late afternoon. He walked to his office without saying a word. It seemed as if he and Jenny were two acquaintances living in the same house. They each had their own space, their own life, their own world and they kept to it. They were cordial to each other, nothing more.

Jenny wanted to ask him where he went last night, but dared not. She feared it would set him off. She waited as long as she could and in the early evening she approached him in his office.

"So, you went out to a club last night? What kind of club is it?"

Johnny raised his brow. "Why?"

"Well curiosity for one thing, and I thought maybe it was something we could talk about and share. We don't talk much anymore."

"Maybe I have run out of things to say. Besides, where I go is my business. I just need to get away some times." Johnny's manner was forceful. He brought up his arms and motioned with his hands to Jenny as he spoke. "I go to a club, alright. I need to unwind and relax. You know the pressure I have been under. When I am at the club, I have a couple of drinks, talk with some of the guys there and catch a little sports on the TVs. It takes my mind off of things. It makes it easier for me to sleep when I come home."

"Are there women there?" Jenny shyly asked.

Johnny didn't like where this was going. Jenny was invading his privacy. He saw her as an intruder and he didn't want her there. "Of course there are women there, so what?"

"I just have a feeling you're seeing someone. If you are, just tell me.

I need to know what's wrong with us so we can fix it together. I'll do whatever you want. I love you and I want this to work."

As far as Johnny was concerned, Jenny had just crossed the line. He wasn't ready to bring up Diamond and his plans. He was not about to reveal anything until he heard from Diamond. He looked at his watch, it was 6:30. "Please, let me read in peace. We can finish this discussion later. Don't worry about fixing me any dinner tonight. I plan on eating out and then going to the club again if that is alright with you."

Ron Crocker sat in his living room with a beer in his hand. He was still in a daze from the events that had transpired a day earlier. His best friend for more than 20 years had been the victim of a con. The worst part of it was his friend refused to believe he had been taken.

Ron was furious, he wanted to find a way to convince Johnny he was the victim of a scam. He knew that Johnny had given the apartment to Diamond, not some friend down on his luck as Johnny had mentioned when making the arrangements with him earlier. Ron thought it over for several minutes. He was the owner. There was no reason he couldn't go over to the apartment and search for some evidence that would corroborate everything he had told Johnny and expose Diamond for what she really was. He knew Diamond would be at the club till 2:00 in the morning. Now was the time to go.

When Ron pulled up at the apartment he was surprised to see a small moving van out front with a trailer to tow a car. Ron walked up to the door and let himself in. He noticed the walls were empty and there were thin shadows where pictures had once hung. It was obvious the apartment was being emptied. He could hear a clamoring of items in the kitchen being put into boxes. He walked into the kitchen and startled Diamond who was furiously packing.

"What are you doing here? How did you find me? Get out, I don't have time for you." Diamond assumed she was in charge and Ron wanted a hook-up.

"Don't you know? I'm your landlord. Your Johnny rents this from me. He told me of an old friend who was in need of help so I obliged him."

"No way, Johnny got this place for me." Diamond became intense.

Everything was falling apart and here was another gap in her plan that she had never imagined.

"You had no idea that "your" Johnny and I have been best friends for years. You didn't take the time to really get to know him, all you saw was a lonely, vulnerable, old man that you could rip-off. So even the best laid plans huh…"

"Stop calling him my Johnny. We have a friendship and he likes to get me things. Nothing more, and there's nothing wrong with that."

"You are such a lying bitch. If that's true, why are you packing? Where are you off to? There's plenty wrong here, you led him on and took advantage of him; now he's in love with you. I'll bet that wasn't supposed to happen was it?"

"Johnny's lost it, he asked me to marry him." Diamond went into the bedroom and got the ring from the dresser. Ron followed her. "Look, here is the ring he bought me." Ron looked at the ring Diamond held out as she stood six feet from him. "I'm getting out of here now, before things get worse."

"You just can't run away and leave him without telling him why."

"You tell him Ron, you tell him it was just a game and he got carried away and now the game is over."

"Ok, get out of town if that's your plan. Take everything here, but leave the ring behind."

"Oh no, the ring is mine, Johnny gave it to me." Diamond opened the top dresser drawer and noticed the 38 revolver amid her lingerie. She pulled out the gun and pointed it at Ron.

"What do you think you are doing? Are you out of you mind? Put that thing down and give me the ring, then I'll leave."

"No Ron, I'm warning you. The ring is mine, now you get out or I'll shoot, I mean it" Ron took a couple of steps closer to Diamond, and she reacted pulling the trigger. The gun went off. Ron dropped to his knees clutching his stomach with blood flowing all over his hands.

"You crazy bitch." Ron moaned as he rolled to his side. Diamond walked over to him and shot him once more in the chest. He was dead.

Johnny stopped at a nearby fast food restaurant for a quick burger and fries. He ate in the car and drove around to kill some time before hooking up with Diamond at the Chaise. While at the Chaise, Johnny put down three scotch and sodas waiting for Diamond. He wondered why she had not come in yet, she was always on the floor by 10:00. Johnny finished his drink and walked over to Sweets who was keeping watch not far from the DJ.

"What time is Diamond supposed to come in tonight?"

"She's not coming in, she called in sick."

"Oh, that's too bad. I hope she's ok."

"I'm sure she is. All the girls call in sick once in a while even though they aren't really sick, you know? They just feel they need a day off, a mental health day. That's probably all it is."

"Thanks." Johnny gave Sweets a thumbs up as he left the club. He got in his car and drove to Diamond's apartment. Johnny almost drove past the apartment in the dark. The streets were empty, no cars, and no lights. The inside lights of the apartment were off as well. Johnny thought maybe Diamond was sick after all and was sleeping.

Johnny knocked on the door, there was no response; he took out his key, let himself in and turned on a light. The apartment looked empty. The pictures were gone, along with the stereo and TV. He went in the kitchen and turned on another light, the cabinets were empty. The couch and love seat were all that remained.

He walked back to the bedroom where Diamond slept and saw a figure in the dark on the floor, not far from the bed. "Diamond!" He called out as he switched on the light. He gasped to see Ron lying in a pool of blood. He noticed the revolver he gave Diamond lying on the floor near Ron and realized she had shot him and vanished. He now accepted the fact he was a pawn in a tragedy of his own creation. He saw himself as Canio in Pagliacci. He could hear the voice of Enrico Caruso singing the powerful cadence: 'Vesti la giubba'. *"(Ridi, Pagliaccio, sul tuo amore infranto! Ridi del duol, che t'avvelena il cor)"* "Laugh, clown, at your broken love! Laugh at the grief that poisons your heart!" Johnny let out a mournful cry, unlike the laugh of Canio, while the tears swelled up in his eyes. Just like Canio, Johnny knew the show was coming to an end.

He left the gun where it was. He walked over to the phone and dialed 911. As he was asked to state the nature of his emergency he said, "I want to report a robbery and a murder."

CHAPTER 25

THE POLICE ARRIVED ON THE SCENE within minutes. There were several squad cars, two ambulances and a gathering of blue uniforms, paramedics, reporters, and photographers along with curious neighbors. It was an unusual event to witness at 12:30 am in that part of town.

LA's finest were busy inside the apartment dusting for prints and taking photos of Ron Crocker from every angle imaginable. Two detectives, John Lawrence and Bruce Erickson were questioning Johnny.

"So tell us again Mr. Bradford, what happened here." Detective Lawrence took notes on his pad.

"I just came by to check on a few things here. I'm getting ready to move in."

"You came to check on a few things at this time of night?" Detective Lawrence looked puzzled.

"Yes, sir. I had just left a club and was on my way home. I wanted to make sure the plumbing issues had been fixed before I started to move the rest of my stuff over."

"What club was that?"

"The Chaise," Johnny replied sheepishly.

"I see," Detective Erickson smirked.

Detective Lawrence asked, "So you came in, walked around and found him there on the floor?"

"Yes, that's right."

"Who is he?"

"That's my landlord and best friend, Ron Crocker. We work together at RayCom."

Detective Lawrence pursued his questioning. "Do you know what he was doing here?"

"Not sure," said Johnny." Maybe he was checking to see that the plumbing work was done."

"Is this your gun?" Detective Erickson held up the revolver with his pencil.

"Yes it is mine." Johnny lowered is head and looked down at Ron.

"What do you think happened here?"

"Isn't it obvious?" Johnny was becoming agitated as his voice rose. "This is a robbery gone wrong. I know you are the detectives but it looks to me like a Ron came in and surprised the thief. My artwork is gone and so is my new TV and stereo system that I just purchased for this place."

"Well, you could be right, but we had to ask. The officer will get all your information and we'll be in touch if we need anything else. Just let us check your hand and clothes for powder burns"

The detectives walked away from Johnny unconvinced with his story. It was reasonable he had not yet moved his possessions into the apartment. That would explain the look of emptiness. It also made sense that the only items taken from the apartment were the artwork, TV, and stereo. What did not make sense was why did he have his gun there and nothing else? The detectives were sure Johnny was not telling them everything. There had to be more to his story.

In the morning, Jenny was putting in her earrings as she finished getting ready for church. She had on a modest, flowered dress that stopped just above her knees. She wore heels without stockings. She knew it would be another hot day in LA. When she came out of the bathroom she was surprised to see Johnny in the bedroom dressed in a suit and tie. Johnny smiled at Jenny and politely asked, "Do you mind if I come to church with you today?"

Jenny was stunned. Johnny had not been to church in years. "Why of course you can. What's the occasion?"

Johnny looked down and shook his head sluggishly. "Ron Crocker was murdered last night."

"Oh no! This is terrible. What happened?"

"The police have little to go on right now. It sounds like he surprised a robber in one of his apartments and was shot."

"Well what does this have to do with you?" There was a worried look on Jenny's face.

"I am the one who found him. I called it in."

"What? That makes no sense. I thought you were at a club?"

"I was. And then I went over to one of Ron's apartments."

"Whatever for?" Jenny was totally confused.

Johnny's lies kept weighing him down. It was if he was sinking in quicksand with each new one he concocted. He could no longer discern between the truth and the lies he had been telling. He couldn't keep things straight anymore and he wondered if the police were satisfied with his story. He was not sure he could remember what he had told them. And now he was putting another lie together.

"Ron was letting me use one of his apartments as a place to get away from distractions and focus on my work. I needed my own private place away from home and work to think things out. I've had too many things on my mind and Ron was good enough to let me use an apartment of his that had been empty for some time."

"Johnny, I don't understand. You have your private office here and no one disturbs you there." Jenny could not believe what she was hearing.

"I know, but lately, I haven't been able to concentrate in there. I don't why, I just know it hasn't been working. I have been feeling like I was on the verge of a breakdown. The police questioned me for some time and then they let me come home." Johnny was convincing. He came off as apologetic in his lying confession.

"There's one more thing and it doesn't look good."

"What's that?" Jenny was becoming nervous, "What more could there be?"

"Ron was killed with my gun."

"How is that possible?" I thought you got rid of that thing ages ago!"

"No, I just recently took it over to the apartment. I wanted it for protection."

"You still had that thing in the house when I asked you to get rid of it? It was still here and the boys could have found it? How could you do that?

You are just lucky that tragedy didn't happen. You know how I hate guns. And now because of your gun, your best friend is dead. I cannot believe this. Come on, we better get to church."

The house was silent the next day. Jenny was still trying to comprehend everything that Johnny had revealed to her the day before. She now felt that the man whom she had been married to for the last 35 years was unrecognizable. Jenny could not believe how her life was unraveling. He husband was going to strip clubs and he was drinking. She wondered if this was some bizarre midlife crisis brought about by the fact that Johnny was not a young man anymore and had lost his confidence. Jenny believed they could work it out and get through this. But now there was a murder in the mix and Johnny could be implicated.

Jenny's thoughts were interrupted when the silence of the house was broken by the sound of the phone ringing. Jenny walked over to the phone and answered it.

"Hello?" Jenny's voice was soft and quiet.

"Mrs, Bradford?"

"Yes."

"This is Detective Lawrence LA police. We spoke with your husband the other day. Is he home?"

"Yes, I'll get him." Jenny found Johnny in his office with an empty glass in his hand. He turned to her and said, "Who's on the phone?"

"It's the police. They want to talk to you." Johnny got out of his chair and walked over to the phone. "Yes detective, what can I do for you?"

"Mr. Bradford, can you come down to the precinct. We have a few more questions. We are trying to clear up a few of the facts and we think you can probably shed some light on the gray areas."

"Yes, I guess I can come down. It won't take long will it?"

"No, probably just an hour, two hours tops."

"OK." Johnny hung up the phone and told Jenny he needed to go to the station. He said he would not be gone long and the detectives needed to clarify some things. As Johnny left the house and drove downtown he tried to remember what he had told the detectives earlier. He had to keep his story straight and consistent. He wondered what facts the police had uncovered. He told himself to remain calm as he pulled into the parking garage on Broadway.

Johnny went into the station, Detectives Lawrence and Erickson greeted him and led him to an interrogation room. Detective Lawrence told Johnny the test for gun powder came up negative but there was another set of prints found in the apartment aside from his, unfortunately no match. Johnny thought they must have been Diamond's and was relieved she hadn't been identified.

Detective Erickson mentioned, "The gun was wiped clean."

"Well that makes sense." Johnny said.

"Where were you Saturday night between 7:00 and 9:00 pm? Detective Lawrence asked.

"I went to the drive through at Bob's Burgers on Seventh and grabbed a bite to eat."

"What time was that exactly?"

"Around 7:30 I think."

"What did you do for the next hour and a half?"

"I drove around up towards Griffith Park."

"Did you stop and talk with anyone?"

"No, I just drove around until I decided to head out to the Chaise. I think I got there at 9:30."

"Well, we checked your story at the Chaise. The owner says you were there until 11:00. He also said you were a regular."

"I don't know what he means by a regular. I have only been there a few times."

"We also talked with some of the neighbors. They didn't notice anything unusual that night, but one of them heard a sound, and couldn't make it out. She thought maybe it was a gunshot around 8:30 but could not be sure. We thought this was interesting, no one remembers seeing you at the apartment at any time, although they do remember a woman. Do you know anything about her?"

Fear overcame Johnny's disposition. He wanted to keep his association and relationship with Diamond out of this. He was sure Diamond shot Ron, he didn't know why, but he had to deny knowing anything about her. All Johnny knew was that in spite of everything that happened, he still loved her.

"Ron told me there had been a women living there before. That's all I know, I never met her."

"We heard you and Ron Crocker got into a fight at work? What was that all about?"

Johnny became tense. Where were they going with this? How did they find these things out so fast?

"It wasn't a fight. It was just we had a difference of opinion about the direction of a certain project at work."

"The way we heard it, you punched him and knocked him down and your boss had to come in and break it up."

Johnny got defensive. "No it wasn't like that at all. I just lost it for a moment. I don't even remember hitting him. It was like I was in a daze. You have no idea how passionate I am about my work."

"We think you were still upset about whatever it was you were arguing about. You knew he was going to be at the apartment and went over there, shot him and made it look like a robbery gone bad."

Johnny started trembling. "No, you've got it all wrong. I didn't kill Ron, I couldn't."

At that point the lieutenant opened the door and walked in. "I think we've heard enough. Arrest him. We'll let the DA take it from here."

Johnny felt the handcuffs snapping on his wrists as he was Mirandized. "I want a lawyer." Johnny shouted as he was led to a cell.

Johnny made his one call to Jenny after he was booked. He told her to contact his boss Al Rogers and see about getting him a lawyer. He told Jenny not to worry and this was a big misunderstanding and everything would work out.

That night was the worst night Johnny had ever spent in his life. He was a prisoner locked up with other criminals and his freedom no longer existed. His cell was a small eight by ten with two bunks in it. There was a metal commode sitting out the open on the floor for when he needed to perform his bodily functions without privacy.

Lights went out at 10:00. He was hungry, he was alone, and he was frightened. He laid on the top bunk of his cell and listed to the harrowing sounds of the night. There were yells, demonic laughter and at times screams. He tried to sleep but his anxiety prevented it from happening. By 11:30 another man was brought into his cell and locked up with him. Johnny did not look to see who it was or speak. He positioned himself silently on his bunk and gradually fell asleep.

By noon the next day Johnny was brought out of his cell and put in another interrogation room. There was a man in a suit with a briefcase sitting there that Johnny didn't recognize.

"I am Richard Jensen, your attorney. Al Rogers has arranged for me to take your case. I have looked over the evidence and it appears to be obviously circumstantial. I do not think they have a leg to stand on but I must warn you, I have seen them get convictions with less. Now you have not given them anything and I want you to keep quiet. Let me do the talking."

"OK, but when can you get me out of here? Don't I get bail?" Johnny was a nervous wreck.

"I am working this, I'll have you out of here soon." Johnny told Richard Jenson all the details of he remembered that he told the police. After an hour of discussion, the Assistant District Attorney knocked on the door. Richard Jensen said to Johnny. "Let's hear him out, let me do all the talking" Jensen walked over to the window and waved two attorneys from the DA's office to enter. As they came in and sat down, the Assistant District Attorney Gerald Clark said, "I am going lay my cards on the table. I have got motive, and I know your client had a fight with the deceased just a day before the murder. There is opportunity, and we have the weapon. Your client has admitted to it being his gun. And he doesn't have an alibi."

"You've got nothing," said Jensen. "My client wasn't seen at the apartment until after the shooting. There are no prints on the gun. You never found powder burns on my client. There were no witnesses. Also someone said there had been a woman living there and they saw her come out around the time of the murder. That sounds like reasonable doubt to me. All you have is a little piece of circumstance and speculation. I am motioning to dismiss on insufficient evidence. You have really jumped the gun this time with your rush to judgement tactics."

Johnny's heart sunk. Someone saw Diamond. He wasn't about to let her be brought into this. She killed Ron, and it didn't matter. All Johnny knew was he loved her, and would do anything to prevent them from connecting her to the murder.

"I think I have enough," replied Clark. "I will take it to a grand jury, they will indict. I'll let a jury decide, I'm going for Man 2."

"It will never happen." Responded Jenson with certainty.

"I have won with less." Clark's arrogance was convincing. Johnny leaned over and whispered in Jensen's ear. Jensen nodded. "What can you offer us?" Jensen asked.

Clark responded, "What's he got to say?"

"Speaking hypothetically of course," said Jensen, "Imagine my client is just going to check on his apartment and see if the plumbing problem was fixed. He sees his landlord there and they start arguing about the problem that had not been resolved the previous day. Tempers begin to flare, both men are passionate about their opinions in this matter. My client goes into the bedroom followed by his landlord, he is worried what his landlord might do and pulls the revolver out of the bedroom dresser in order to frighten his landlord and protect himself. His hand is shaky as he points the gun, having never pointed a gun at anyone and then the gun accidentally goes off twice, killing Mr. Crocker. My client is scared and quickly leaves the scene but realizes later what he must do and calls the police after he returns to the scene. This is indeed a tragedy and sparks of innocent by virtue of self-defense."

"That's a great story Mr. Jensen, but I don't see any self-defense here. Where was the imminent threat? Where was the other weapon? There's nothing to indicate Crocker had shown any violence whatsoever. The story is not plausible."

"You might not think it's plausible, but I'll see that a jury does. You know I can," said Jensen convincingly. "I know you can do better than Man 2."

Clark continued, "Like you, I don't want to waste a jury's time or the tax payer's money. You're right, this is a tragedy and your client made a bad decision and needs to be punished for it. The law demands it. Involuntary Manslaughter, five to ten years. That's my offer. Take it or take your chances with a jury."

Johnny and his attorney whispered back and forth a several times. Jensen kept shaking his head but Johnny remained firm in what he would accept. Jensen looked back at Clark and said, "I think my client is making a mistake, we'll take the deal, prepare the paperwork."

CHAPTER 26

JOHNNY WAS IN JAIL. DUE TO the inspired eloquence of attorney Richard Jensen at allocution and the fact that Johnny had plead guilty showing much remorse during sentencing, the judge ordered Johnny be incarcerated at the Seventh Street Regional Jail. This was much better than going to state prison in Lancaster. Here Jenny, other family members and friends could visit Johnny without making a two to three hour drive, although no one had even made the twenty minute drive.

Like most prisoners, Johnny was unhappy in jail, but he adjusted well. He got along with his cellmate Leon Jones, a young man of 35, who held up a convenience store. Both men kept to themselves and agreed they would keep their noses clean and do their time.

Jenny was lost without Johnny at home. She couldn't get used to the idea he was not there. She still made enough dinner for two in the evenings out of habit. She found herself saying she was going to bed at night even though there was no one to hear her. There were nights when she would lie in her bed and cry herself to sleep.

It was nearly a month before Jenny found the strength to visit Johnny. When Johnny was told he had a visitor, he was in shock. Nobody came to see him since his incarceration. He felt abandoned, but he felt he deserved it. Guilt followed his every step while a cloud of remorse hung over his head. His eyes beamed as he came to the window and saw Jenny. He smiled and picked up the phone.

"Well this is a nice surprise. What brings you down here?"

"Oh Johnny, I didn't want you to think I'd forgotten you. I'm sorry it took me so long."

"That is alright. I would not have blamed you if you never came after what I have put you through. I am the one that is sorry."

"Oh Johnny," she fought back the tears, "I hope they are treating you well. No one's being mean to you are they?"

"No they treat me just fine. I don't give anyone reason for trouble and the inmates here leave me alone. I get along well with the guards so that makes life easier. Say did you find that manila folder I left on my office desk at the house? It gives you all the information about our finances, bills, how I pay for things and how you can monitor everything from the computer."

"I saw two envelopes like that on your desk. One said instructions but there was nothing on the other one."

"Get the one that says instructions. That tells you everything you need to know. If it confuses you, check with Maddy's husband Jim. He's pretty computer savvy. I am sure he can get you through it."

"Ok, I will go read the instructions and try and muddle through. You are right, Jim is knowledgeable when it comes to computers, unlike me."

"Don't sell yourself short girl. You have never been properly trained. I hold myself to blame for that." Johnny coughed several times.

"Johnny, are you ok? Jenny expressed concern over Johnny's coughing.

"Yes I am fine, I'm not used to talking this much and my throat gets dry when I do."

"Maybe you should see a doctor. Tell them you need to see a doctor. What is in the other envelope?"

"That is for you too, divorce papers. I have already filled them out and signed them. You can just go ahead and sign them in front of an attorney whenever you like. I've left you everything. Give Richard Jensen a call if you need help. I'm sure he can refer someone."

"Johnny," there was alarm in Jenny's voice as she spoke. "I don't want a divorce, is that what you want?"

"I just want what's best for you."

"You are what's best for me. You are my world, you have always been that. I cannot imagine life without you. I will wait for you. Say it's ok Johnny, say it's ok, I love you."

"I am so sorry Jenny. I never wanted to hurt you. I've been foolish and selfish, and you've been the best wife a man could ever ask for. I have proved unworthy of you and your love. I don't deserve you and I hope someday you can forgive me."

The guard walked up to Johnny, "Times up. Let's go back." Johnny stood up and walked back to his cell thinking of the irony listening to Jenny pouring out her heart, and describing herself as the wife Johnny had always wanted but had never seen. Jenny remained at the window sobbing profusely.

Johnny kept himself busy while in jail. During the first three months of his incarceration, he read eight books and lost 15 pounds. He grew a short, stubbly, beard so he wouldn't have to shave every day. Even though it was sparse, he felt it gave him a more rugged look and hid his boyish face. Jenny continued visited him every Tuesday and talked about Maddy, the boys, how they were growing and everything she had been doing. She commented on his beard and never brought up the subject of divorce. She had torn up the papers and burned them; she never told Johnny.

Johnny continued to cough more frequently each time they met. He remained consistent using the same excuse each time Jenny visited him. Jenny insisted he see a doctor, Johnny promised her he would but never did.

Johnny had another visitor during his stay, Joe Bordan from RayCom. Johnny was pleased to see Joe, he wanted all the news from RayCom.

"We delivered the X-Lab prototype on time. It is a huge win for the company as you can imagine." Johnny gave two thumbs up.

"What about the ProSoft contract?"

"Johnny, you aren't going to believe this. The company disclosed they signed the contract five months ago and had set up a partnership with them. Dana Pulley joined their team and was given a promotion and a technical lead position."

"You are kidding me right?"

"Nope, and there's more. You remember Cord?"

"Sure, what about him?" Johnny sounded disgusted.

"He got all the credit, Al Rogers said that through Cord's leadership, Dana's solution became a reality, and he was promoted to director!"

"Well if that doesn't that beat all. I guess Ron was correct in his assessment about business" Johnny shook his head and muttered, "Cord really has had the last laugh. He gets the promotion and I get prison. I guess life really is a story told by an idiot, full of noise and emotional disturbance but devoid of meaning."

"What are you talking about Johnny?"

"It's Shakespeare, never mind."

"Oh and one more thing you will not believe, Dana and I are now an item."

"No kidding? You and dangerous Dana?" Johnny laughed and then coughed several times. Joe's face was full of concern. "You ok Johnny? I know you didn't kill Ron. I know you; who are you covering for and why?"

"Nonsense. Not another word Joe. I am the reason Ron is dead. It is irrelevant who pulled the trigger. I am the cause of everyone's misery. An unforgiveable crime was committed and justice and society demand someone should be punished, that someone is me. I am the one who must repent, if that's even possible. I only hope God can forgive me." Johnny coughed several times more.

"Johnny, you sound terrible. You need to take care of yourself" There was a tap on the window, "Time," a commanding voice decreed. Johnny stood up and walked back to his cell.

It had been seven months since Diamond left Los Angeles, she settled in Las Vegas. The only thing different in her lifestyle was the location. She walked along the sand, barefoot with her flip-flops in her hand along the faux beach at Mandalay Bay. There were umbrellas and beach chairs lined up as far as the eye could see. She wore a scanty blue bikini and had a lace towel wrapped around her waste in such a fashion to create a slit up her tanned right leg. Diamond walked over to the cabana area and caught sight of a solitary gentleman who she perceived was in need of company. Another potential victim was lining up in her sights.

Diamond assessed he looked 50 and was approximately six feet tall. It was hard to be accurate since he was sitting in his chair. He was lightly tan. His salt and pepper hair was dignified and well groomed; the grey area surrounding his temples touched his ears, while the back stopped just above his collar. He orange designer swimsuit went well with his body tone. There was a flat screen TV attached to the top inside of his cabana presenting a sporting event. Next to his chair was an ice bucket with a bottle of champagne. There was also another chair with a newspaper on it.

Diamond was not about to miss her chance. She walked up to him with her glossed lips smiling, "You look like you need a friend. Mind if I join you?"

The gentleman was no fool, he knew a player when he saw one and he was wise to the game as well.

"Sure, come on in. Would you like a drink?"

"I'd love one, it's beastly hot out there. I do enjoy walking on the sand, but the heat wears me down."

The gentleman poured her some of the chilled Montaudon Brut. "I'm Andre, who are you?"

"I'm Ruby." Diamond took a sip. "Ooh, this is so refreshing, and what flavor. I love the tickling bubbles." Diamond was baiting the hook.

"Ruby huh, I'll be you're really a diamond in the rough."

"Aren't you the clever one!" laughed Diamond. "It's not like I haven't heard similar lines, but I like it just the same."

"Are you a local?"

"Yes, I'm a waitress here. My shift doesn't start until this evening so I come down to the fake beach just to kill some time. Where are you from?"

"LA. We have real beaches down there you know."

Diamond laughed. "Oh I'd love to go to California, I've never been. I want to go to a real beach and try surfing. So what's new in LA?" She asked.

"Well I have the Times here if you are interested. One of the stories that caught my eye was about this guy who accidently shot his friend over a work dispute. Crazy stuff. The guy copped a plea and went to a local jail. They gave him three years."

Diamond looked nervous. "Yeah that sounds crazy alright."

"But here is what's really nuts. He had not been in there long and died."

"What? Really? Can I see that paper?" Diamond asked hesitantly.

Andre handed her the paper. She saw the article that Andre had mentioned. It was Johnny. He had died of pneumonia after being in jail only six months. "Poor old fool; poor old fool." Diamond spoke softly under her breath.

"Ruby did you say something?"

"Um, how about another drink? Then what do you think about going back to the hotel for some cheese cake and coffee topped with Baileys Irish Cream? And then, who knows?"

"Ruby, you've talked me into it." Andre stood up and helped Diamond out of her chair. She took his arm as they walked along the sand back to the hotel. She tried not to think about Johnny, after all, it wasn't her fault, and she didn't make him confess. She put Johnny out of her mind while tugging Andre's arm and though to herself, "Victory."

Printed in the United States
By Bookmasters